THE HOMETOWN
hoax

HEATHER THURMEIER

Entangled Publishing, LLC
2614 South Timberline Road
Suite 109
Fort Collins, CO 80525
Visit our website at www.entangledpublishing.com.

Lovestruck is an imprint of Entangled Publishing, LLC.

Edited by Alethea Spiridon Hopson
Cover design by Heather Howland
Cover art from iStock

Manufactured in the United States of America

First Edition November 2015

To my Readers,
This one is for you. Thank you for giving your time to my words, for falling in love with my characters, and for going on this journey with me from Chapter One to The End. Every day I'm lucky to do a job that I love. By reading my books, you allow me to continue writing and living my dreams.
~ Heather

Chapter One

Even the highway signs were counting down until the moment of her unwanted return. Twenty-two miles until she had to defend her choice to live in the city. Twenty-two minutes until she had to convince her family that her *fake* boyfriend Richard, who was currently back in the city and too busy to leave for the week, was *real* and serious. There was no possible way she could move back to Cutter's Creek.

Tessa Cutter would rather drink green smoothies every day for the rest of her life than move back to the town that barely let her leave in the first place. A place with people she couldn't trust to keep her best interests at heart when her wishes contradicted theirs.

Nestled in the foothills of the Appalachian Mountains in West Virginia, the place had more charm than most small towns. And it wasn't that small really. Cutter's Creek was actually on the larger side of the small town scale with a few thousand year-round residents as well as another couple thousand seasonal ones. In the summer they got the fishermen and hunters, and in the winter they got the skiers.

Yet, even with the fluctuating population helping to bring in people from around the world, the place still felt stagnant. Tessa had always wanted more. She wanted to see somewhere other than her little town, experience other places, and paint them all on canvas. But that wasn't the only reason she had to leave. During her college years away, she'd had a serious long-distance relationship with her high school boyfriend. Well, she'd been serious. Zack had seemed serious and a touch controlling. He liked to tell her about all the great things she could do in town if she'd stop "playing" with her paints at college. He'd even gone so far as to get her a job when she came home over the summer, hoping to entice her into staying with a fine career in greeting card retail.

Working for Sue-Ellen had been terrible, but not as bad as learning from the local greeting card patrons that Zack had been cheating on her the whole time. Seemed the whole town knew and no one wanted to tell her. Why would they when it would only make her want to leave more?

She'd made a vow to leave Cutter's Creek as soon as possible so that she'd finally have her independence. She'd done the only thing she could do—she'd moved to New York City and hoped to make it big enough that she could support herself and live anywhere she wanted. After a year, it still hadn't happened. She barely had enough to pay her rent each month, and she was sharing a place with three roommates. Not exactly her ideal living situation.

When she became a famous artist, her paintings would hang in galleries around the world. She'd finally have a legitimate excuse for why she couldn't move back home to Nowheresville and become a housewife and baby maker, like her family wanted. Until then, she had to stay strong and stand her ground.

And create a fake boyfriend to shut up her family.

Squealing tires and red brake lights up ahead interrupted her thoughts. The car in front of her slammed on their brakes so suddenly that it fishtailed between the colored lines. She thumped on her own brakes, barely hanging on to control of the vehicle, but she was too close to the other car and would smash into the back bumper in another millisecond if she didn't swerve around it fast. Without thinking about the possible repercussions, she twisted the steering wheel sharply to the right, running onto the shoulder far faster than she was comfortable with.

Gravel clinked against the undercarriage while the tires skidded like a skipping stone on a calm lake. Her brakes jolted and shuddered as they tried to find purchase on the loose ground. A second later, the front right corner of the bumper made contact with the metal guardrail. The sound of metal crumpling echoed through the mountains as her car came to rest dangerously close to the edge of the cliff.

A trembling began in her fingertips and worked its way through her arms, down her torso, and all the way to her toes, which were still pressed against the pedal. She forced one hand from the steering wheel and slowly pushed the shifter into park then turned the key in the ignition to off. Not that her car could go anywhere anyway. By the amount of steam currently seeping out from under the hood, it would be a miracle if the thing moved again without the assistance of a tow truck. She wasn't about to try. Good thing it was a rental and would hopefully be covered by insurance.

She stumbled out of the car to examine the damage. It was bad, but thankfully hadn't been hard enough or fast enough to do any permanent, unfixable damage to the car or her. The airbags hadn't even deployed.

"Are you okay?"

The man who came up beside her was tall and fairly

light haired, dirty blond. He had bright blue eyes that almost sparkled in the late-afternoon sunshine and a sprinkle of stubble dusted his jaw, giving him an even more concerned expression than he would have had with only his lips pressed into a tight line.

He squeezed her shoulders with his large, strong hands. "Are you hurt? Do you know what day it is?"

A mystery man had come to rescue her as if she were starring in a princess movie. She shook her head, clearly not thinking straight. She didn't believe in fairytale endings from the corny movies she watched as a kid. Sure, those kinds of things happened in real life; that wasn't the issue. She just didn't think her life required a man to have a happily ever after.

Nope. She only needed her sketchbook, a few pencils, and a ticket to somewhere new and amazing. Not a man who would tie her down and keep her in one place forever. The only person she could trust with her happiness in life was herself. However, that didn't mean she couldn't appreciate the hunky guy in front of her currently offering his assistance.

"I'm fine," she said. "I didn't hit my head or anything."

"Good. You're okay." He let go of her shoulders and ran his hands through his hair, turning toward her rental car and giving it the once over. He exhaled with a whistle. "That doesn't look good. What happened?"

"I was driving and suddenly the car in front of me slammed on their brakes for no reason." She pointed up the road, seeing the moment replay in her mind. "Then I had to slam on mine too and aim for the shoulder so I wouldn't hit them. What kind of idiot hits the brakes like that on the highway?"

Now that she looked at the other stopped car, the one the hunky stranger got out of, it looked sort of familiar. Of course, how different did one set of taillights look from another?

"The kind of driver who is paying attention and wants to avoid killing the deer that jumped into the road. I heard squealing tires, but I thought they were mine. Then when I heard the crunch of metal, I knew it was someone else."

"That was you? You're the one who almost got me killed?" Her voice came out shriller than she intended, but she couldn't stop her tone anymore than she could stop the anger rising inside of her.

"You were the one tailgating and obviously not paying attention. What were you doing? Checking your makeup in the mirror? Texting your bestie?"

"Did you just say bestie?" Surely he hadn't. "Real men do not use words like *bestie*."

"Are you avoiding the question?" He arched an eyebrow.

She tucked a few loose strands of hair behind her ear before hiking up her jeans—they always managed to wiggle down her hips lower than she wanted, giving her that unappealing droopy-ass syndrome—then smoothed the hem of her tailored button-up blouse back into place. "Just because I want to be put together does not mean I'm superficial enough to be more concerned about my makeup than the cars around me. And I don't believe in texting while driving. I can barely text and walk at the same time. I'm not stupid enough to try it while behind the wheel."

She folded her arms across her chest, challenging him to accuse her of something else ridiculous. "Maybe you're the one who wasn't paying attention and therefore only narrowly avoided killing Bambi. Don't blame your bad driving skills on me." The last word came out so forcefully her chest heaved as she breathed in.

"I didn't do anything wrong. I didn't even have to stop to make sure you were okay, but I did, because I'm a nice guy." He crossed his arms to mirror hers. His once concerned expression had been replaced by one of complete and total pissed-off-ness.

Ditto, buddy.

"Well, thank you much for your kindness, but I'm fine, so you can go." She turned around and forced her annoyance into the background. Being pissed off wouldn't help her get her rental car moving again. Instead, she climbed behind the wheel and twisted the key in the ignition. Nothing happened. It didn't even click.

"Great," she muttered. Maybe if she gave it a little gas and then tried again.

"I don't think you should do that," the guy said, tapping on her driver's side window.

She glared at him and opened her door since she couldn't roll down her window without power. What did he know about anything? "And why not?"

"There's a puddle of liquid pooling beneath your car, and it might be important. What if your engine is damaged and it sparks when you try to get it running again? What if that liquid is flammable?"

Good point. She didn't feel like becoming a toasted marshmallow today, but did she want to admit Mr. Accident Causer was right? Nope. "I have to get it started somehow. I can't leave it here. Got any better ideas?"

"We could call a tow truck and have it taken to town. Cutter's Creek isn't too far from here." He pointed down the road in the direction they'd both been heading.

She didn't need reminding of how close she was to home. She knew. It was like her body was finely tuned to the area. She knew every landmark, outcropping of rocks, and overlook. She wasn't happy to be back, but at least her brother was nearby and he could fix her car. Cheap auto repair was one good thing about being home, possibly the only good thing. The other side of the coin was that by morning the whole town would know she was home and had almost driven herself off a mountain. She could already hear the comments about how the city had changed her.

Just another thing she disliked about coming home—constant rumors and gossip.

Good thing she was headed directly to meet her family at the campground and not into town. With any luck, she'd be able to avoid seeing anyone but family for the entire week before she left again.

Admitting he was right, she pulled out her phone only to find it didn't have a signal. *Shit. The dead zone.* She'd forgotten how these mountains always cut off her signal at random points along this stretch of road. It was another one of the annoying things about being out in the middle of nowhere. How would she get an email response from the galleries she still had outstanding applications with if she couldn't get a signal to check her messages? The week kept getting worse.

"I don't have a signal here. Can you check your phone?"

He did and shook his head. "Me either. Must be these mountains getting in the way of the cell towers. Grab whatever you need to take with you and hop in with me." He motioned for her to follow him back to his car.

"I'm not going anywhere with you. You could be a murderer."

He laughed. "Really? First you accuse me of being a bad driver trying to take down Bambi, and subsequently you, and now I'm a murderer. You think highly of well-meaning strangers who are trying to help you; though why I'm still trying is beyond me."

"Well, you could be," she said weakly, feeling her cheeks warm with embarrassment. She should've kept that murderer comment to herself. "I don't know you. You could be some psycho waiting to have your way with me." The heat in her cheeks deepened. Somehow that came out sounding a lot more sexual than she intended.

He chuckled again. "I assure you, if I wanted you dead, you would've been by now. And if I wanted to have my way with you, I'd save that for a time when you'd appreciate it, not when we're stuck on the side of the road. Now, you're free to stay here and wait for your signal to come back, or you can ride with me and I'll drop you off wherever you want so you can get your car fixed. Choice is yours, but I'm late getting where I need to go as it is, so I'm leaving, with or without you." He stalked off to his car without a backward glance.

Tessa chewed the inside of her cheek, debating. Risk her safety but get to town where she could deal with her car? Or wait by the side of the road for someone she knew to come along? Of course, they'd been out here a while already and not a single car had passed. She could be here for hours without someone she knew finding her. Better to risk it with the stranger.

"Fine. Wait up," she called before he got into his car. There wasn't much she needed to take with her, just her handbag and small suitcase. As she settled herself into the passenger seat, the pit of uneasiness in her stomach blossomed. On second thought, hanging out on the side of the road might be better than dealing with her family and their persistent questions and not so subtle hints about moving home.

"I'm Logan, by the way. Logan Ridley. You know, so I'm not a stranger anymore. And you are?"

"Tessa." Whenever people around here heard her full name, they instantly associated her with the rest of the family. Not that her family was bad. They were great people actually—kind, warm, and friendly. Along with being meddling, busy-bodied know-it-alls who all thought they knew what she needed in her life to be happy better than she knew herself. She loved her family deeply, but damn it they could be annoying as hell.

"Just Tessa?" he asked with a quick glance toward her.

"Eyes on the road. One close call is enough for the day, thanks. And yeah, just Tessa."

One of the things she liked the most about living in New York City was being anonymous. She didn't miss living in a town where everyone knew her and what she was doing every day. In the city if she wanted to grab coffee from the corner café in her jammies, no one batted an eyelash. Try that in town and it would make the front page of the *Cutter's Creek Gazette*.

This guy didn't look like anyone she remembered from town, so there was a good chance he was passing through. Although if he had half a brain, he'd still put her name together with the town.

"Okay then. Where can I drop you off?" he asked.

"Miller's campground, just outside of Cutter's Creek, if that's not out of your way," she added, hoping to sound a little less grouchy. She did appreciate him driving her to her family instead of leaving her on the side of the road like he could've easily done, but that didn't mean she excused him for being the root of the situation to begin with.

"I'm headed there myself. How strange."

"And convenient." *Murderer? Psychopath? Stop it. Just another camper like you. Relax.*

"No, just coincidence. I was in Stony Brook for the morning taking care of some business before meeting friends out at the campsite. Guess you'll have to share the campground with a murderous, bad-driving lunatic, huh?" He chuckled. She didn't.

"I don't think that's funny, but it's a good thing you'll be nearby in case the rental place wants to talk to the guy who ruined my car. They might need a statement or something to verify the facts once I call to tell them what happened."

"I'll give them my side of the story if you insist, but I'm not taking the blame for your shitty driving."

"You think you're blameless in this situation?" How could he be so ignorant?

"You think *you're* blameless?" he echoed.

"It was *your* fault," she said.

"You were the one driving your car. Not me. Therefore, I can't be held accountable for your actions." His voice rose as he took the corner into Miller's Campground a little too fast, gravel spinning out from under the tires.

She gripped the dashboard and the side of her seat. "You're really proving your point about being a good driver."

"And you're doing a good job of proving how irritating you can be. What site can I drop you at?"

"Fifteen."

He skidded to a stop by a sign that read *Cabins 12-17* and leaned back his head onto the headrest, belly laughing. He wiped his watering eyes and shook his head. "This is great. Amazing."

"I'll get out here. Thanks for the lift." She went to grab the door handle but stopped as the car inched forward again, then turned up the gravel road leading toward the cabins.

"I'm going this way anyway. I'll drive you."

"You don't have to. I'll walk the rest of the way so you can get where you're going. I'll find you if I need you for the rental car insurance."

"You won't have to look far," he said, pulling into a parking spot next to her parents' vehicle.

"What do you mean? What cabin are you staying in?" Hopefully it wasn't too close by. She wanted him near enough so she could have him report about the accident, but not so close she'd have to see him around. He might be cute, but he'd also rubbed her the wrong way basically every second since they'd met.

"I'm not sure exactly. I was told to meet everyone here."

"Here as in Miller's Campground?" Surely he didn't

mean what she thought he meant.

He faced her, an expression of sheer disbelief on his face. "Here as in cabin fifteen where I'm meeting my friend Travis."

"As in Travis Baker my brother-in-law?" Was Logan the friend of the family they'd mentioned inviting? What were the odds of that?

"And you must be the wild and free-spirited Tessa Cutter I've heard so much about. This is not how I imagined meeting you."

"Shut the hell up," she whispered almost speechless. How could she possibly have luck this bad?

"Looks like we'll be spending the week together. Good thing we got off to such a great start. First impressions and all that. Should make the week lots of fun."

He laughed and got out of the car, grabbed his bag from the trunk, and threw it over his shoulder. "What are you waiting for? I'm sure your family would love to hear all about our little adventure today."

There wasn't a doubt in her mind that they would. Hopefully, they'd get it out of their system quickly then Logan could go hang out with Travis on the lake fishing for the entire week, if there was any justice in the universe, and she could find somewhere on dry land to be—as far away from Logan as possible.

Chapter Two

"You're here," her mother said, hugging Tessa, who looked reluctant to hug her back. "Who is this young man with you?"

"Travis's friend Logan," Tessa said.

"I'm glad you brought him with you, Tessa-bear."

"I didn't bring him. We just sort of ended up together."

Tessa practically growled at the use of her nickname. Clearly, she didn't like being called Tessa-bear. He'd have to remember that the next time he needed to piss her off. He clenched his jaw and bit back a chuckle.

Logan smiled politely and held out his hand when her mother turned her attention to him, but instead of accepting his proffered hand, she scooped him into a tight embrace.

"It's nice to have you here, Logan. We're so glad you could join us."

"Thank you for having me, Mrs. Cutter, and for the warm welcome."

"Any friend of Travis's is a friend of the whole family. You can call me Martha." Her mother ushered them into the main cabin, closing the door behind them.

He glanced over to Tessa. She didn't look as if she agreed with that statement. At least not where he was concerned. He set down his bags inside the door. At some point he'd ask where to put them, but that seemed less important at the moment then saying hello to the rest of the family who were currently seated in the large combination living room and dining room.

The cabin was more luxurious on the inside than he'd expected. Large beams, that looked as if they'd once come directly out of the forest surrounding them, were the anchors of the walls at each corner and midpoint. Smaller, yet still substantial, logs made up the majority of the walls and ceiling adding a rustic edge to the luxury. The oversized fireplace was clearly the focal point of the room and definitely a place he could imagine spending the chilly evenings in front of with a scotch in hand. The caramel-colored leather furniture and an oak dining table that could easily seat sixteen completed the space.

"How funny that the two of you managed to show up at the exact same time." If he wasn't mistaken, Martha sent a knowing glance toward Tessa's family. Or maybe he was suddenly nervous at being the odd one out in the room.

"We ended up coming together," he said. He didn't miss the way Tessa's eyes grew larger at the comment. Had her mind just wandered somewhere dirty like his had? Surely he'd misunderstood her reaction. There was no way the woman who'd argued with him for the last hour would go anywhere near the naughty section of her brain where he was concerned. Or maybe she had. Stranger things could happen—like getting into an almost-accident with someone only to end up on vacation with them.

With her shoulder-length, light brown hair, hazel eyes, and full lips, she was definitely attractive. Tall and leggy didn't hurt either. He quite enjoyed the curves filling out her skinny jeans. While living in New York City, he'd dated his fair share of walking sticks, and he'd discovered he much more enjoyed the softer suppleness of curves to the slim, bordering on bony, figures of more weight-conscious women.

Tessa had some good curves.

Too bad those curves came attached to a spitfire personality that was currently spitting fire in his direction. If he wasn't careful and pissed her off anymore, he'd run a serious risk of getting burned. He couldn't believe this was the same girl he'd been longing to meet every time Travis mentioned her over the years.

"Oh? I didn't think you two knew each other."

"We don't," Tessa said, slipping off her knee-high boots and squeezing into a spot on the couch. She pulled her legs up underneath her and accepted the glass of red wine her father offered. After a rather long gulp, she continued. "He forced me off the road and almost killed me."

"He what?" her father Joe said, retaking his seat by the fireplace.

"Sounds like a good story," Travis said, walking in from the kitchen.

Sally, Travis's wife and Tessa's older sister, grinned and patted the spot next to her. "Got here just in time for the fireworks."

"I did not almost kill you. Tessa is exaggerating a touch."

"She has a tendency to be dramatic," Sally said.

"I am *not* dramatic." Her voice came out in a high-pitched squeak that would have made a dog's eardrums bleed.

"You'll get used to it if you're around enough," Travis said with a wink in her direction.

Logan tried not to play into their banter, but it was hard when she clearly was being dramatic. He decided to stick to the facts instead. "I avoided a deer in the road, and Tessa barely avoided me by hitting the guardrail instead."

"Is your car okay?" James asked, looking concerned. "Wait. Did you buy a car without consulting me first?"

"No, my car is not okay. I left it on the side of the road. Something leaked out of it and the front right side was kind of crumpled. And no I didn't cheat on you with another car guy. It's a stupid rental. One that hopefully won't cost too much to fix."

"Why didn't you say something right away? I'll send one of my guys out to tow it to the shop." He got up with his cell phone in hand and wandered out of the living room to make the call. Thank goodness the cabin got cell service, at least at the moment.

"Are you both okay?" Sally asked. "I'm assuming you are since you're sitting here and not in a hospital somewhere."

"We're fine. It wasn't a big deal." Logan stretched, twisting one way and then the other. The accident hadn't bothered him, but Tessa was stressing him out, and his body seemed to be tensing up in response.

"Says the guy who didn't hit the guardrail." She huffed and crossed her arms.

"Says the girl who needs to get over it already." He leveled her with a look that would have scared Superman but she didn't waver.

The room went silent as he locked gazes with Tessa. Damn her eyes were gorgeous. An ever-changing mix of blue, green, gray, and brown depending on how the light hit them. They almost seemed to glow. Or maybe that was her annoyance shining brightly.

Tessa's mother broke the silence, her cheerful voice cutting through the tension between them as if it didn't exist. "I thought we might have to hold dinner for you two but here you are. Together already. Funny how things sometimes seem to sort themselves out for us, almost as if fate steps in the way."

"The only thing in the way was Logan's car," Tessa mumbled under her breath but still loud enough for his ears.

"Actually, *Tessa-bear*," he said with special emphasis on her nickname, "the deer was in the way."

"I'll finish up with dinner. Why don't you two get yourselves a drink and settle in. I'm sure you could both use one after the excitement of the day."

Logan poured himself a scotch, not a bad vintage either, and Tessa another glass of wine. He filled hers a little more than he normally would, hoping the effects of the alcohol would take the edge off of her personality so they could finally get past their accident.

"Trying to get me drunk?" she asked accepting the drink.

"Would it help you like me more?"

"Probably not, but it wouldn't hurt either. Miracles could happen. Bottoms up." She raised her glass in a toasting motion then took a long sip.

The rest of the room laughed at their exchange while he seated himself next to Joe, hoping he'd find some way to connect with him so he'd be able to fit in.

"You got off on the wrong foot with my daughter, didn't you?"

"Seems so. She'll get over it after a good night's sleep though, right?"

"If you're lucky."

"And if I'm not?"

"Let's just say Tessa has a long memory, and she's not afraid to use it when she needs to make a point or get her way."

"Great. Any tips on how to smooth things over with her? I'd like to relax and enjoy this week with your family, not be the source of a week-long feud."

"It might not seem like it, but I think you're doing a good

job of it already. Tessa's a strong-willed girl, and she loves to have someone to argue with."

"So I've got that one quality perfected. I can be her verbal sparring partner. Sounds fun. And irritating."

Tessa's mother wandered out of the kitchen with a tray of lasagna. "Dinner's ready."

Logan hesitated, standing and stretching slowly to allow everyone else to get to the table ahead of him. As the newcomer to the group, he didn't know where people normally sat and since he'd already pissed off one Cutter, he didn't want to accidentally piss off another. A few moments later, everyone was seated except him, so he took the one spot left—right beside Tessa.

He figured with the obvious tension between them, the family would arrange it so that they could be as far away from each other as possible. Instead, they were shoulder to shoulder. Not that Tessa seemed to notice. Or if she did, she did a brilliant job of ignoring him.

"So, sis, when are you moving home? The sooner you do, the sooner Mom and Dad will stop bugging me to find a nice girl to married before it's too late." James shoveled a forkful of lasagna into his mouth and chewed noisily. "Like I'll have any trouble getting a wife when I'm ready."

"What girl could resist you with your stellar table manners?" Sally rolled her eyes.

"I'm not moving back," Tessa said, her voice quiet and controlled but with a hint of determination in it. "I moved to New York and I'm staying there. Well, at least until I head off to somewhere else. I'm thinking I'll go to San Francisco next, paint the Golden Gate Bridge and the bay. Maybe I'll even paint the redwoods."

"You paint?" Logan asked.

"Yes, and sketch. I've even dabbled in sculpture once or twice but I don't care for it."

An image of her molding soft clay in her hands flashed through his mind and his gaze drifted to where her fingers stroked a path in the condensation on the outside of her wine glass. The combination was oddly arousing.

"You know those redwoods are teaming with spiders, right?" Sally asked.

"As I was saying, I'll paint the trees from a safe distance, like maybe from Oregon." She bit her lower lip, looking around sheepishly.

Everyone laughed.

"Before you ask, yes, I'm afraid of spiders too," she said.

"Good to know, especially while camping in the woods where I'm sure there are hundreds of spiders per square inch."

"I choose not to hear you right now," Tessa said, smirking. It was the first sign of humor and lightheartedness he'd seen from her. Maybe she was finally warming up to him and forgetting about the accident. He liked her more laid-back side. A girl with a sense of humor was a good thing. Maybe a week with Tessa wouldn't be so terrible after all.

"You know you can paint anywhere in the world and still have your home base here in Cutter's Creek," Joe said. He was a man of few words it seemed, letting everyone else do most of the talking, but when he spoke, the rest of the family listened. "It would be nice to have you home with us when you're not working."

Tessa sighed and dropped her fork, letting it clang onto the plate. "I have a boyfriend, a serious one. I couldn't possibly move back now."

Damn. A boyfriend.

"A boyfriend? Since when?" Her mother fired questions at her so quickly he thought he might have to duck and cover. "What's his name? Why can't he move here with you if he's so serious about this relationship?"

"We met a little while ago on the subway. He's a finance

guy… On Wall Street." She took a sip of her wine and Logan noticed her gaze dart around the table. "His name is Richard…Stroker…"

"Stroker? As in Bram? Are you dating a vampire?" Sally asked, giggling.

"That would be Stoker, actually, but close," Logan said.

"Stroker…man…" Tessa took another sip of wine. More like a gulp.

"Strokerman? That's even worse," Mary, Tessa's younger sister, said.

James turned in his chair and stared at Tessa. "So you're dating a guy named Dick Strokerman?"

The entire table laughed except for Tessa. Logan almost felt bad, except that the guy's name was too funny to ignore. That couldn't be his real name. No parents were that cruel, were they?

"He prefers Richard, and if you ever meet him, that's what you'll call him. Got it?" She glared at each member of the family.

"Why didn't Richard join you this week if you two have suddenly gotten serious?"

Logan might be new to the family, but even he could hear the suspicion in Martha's voice. If her own mother didn't believe her about this guy, then he was right in feeling the same way. Something about Tessa's body language didn't ring true. Not that what her body was doing or not doing should mean anything to him either way.

Regardless of whether or not he found her attractive, and regardless of whether or not he found her temper and feisty personality a challenge that intrigued him, if she said she had a boyfriend, then that was that. Travis had made a point, multiple times, about how his *single* sister-in-law Tessa would be on this camping trip, but apparently she'd gone and gotten herself a boyfriend without telling anyone. Now that she was taken, he wouldn't step on anyone's toes, even if said anyone had a ridiculous fake-sounding name like Dick Strokerman and had decided to stay home and work instead of joining his good-looking girlfriend for a week in the woods away from life's regular distractions.

"Because he's very busy at work right now and couldn't get away," she said, raising her chin slightly.

"Do you have a picture of him at least?" Mary asked.

Tessa bit her lower lip and shifted in her seat. If he wasn't mistaken, she suddenly looked nervous. "Um, sure. Let me see if I can find one on my phone."

He leaned back in his chair. The notion of having to gush over some picture of her boyfriend made his stomach feel like he'd eaten bad sushi. She flicked her finger across her phone screen repeatedly. Why was it taking her so long to find a photo? Surely she had taken plenty of pictures with her new, serious boyfriend, hadn't she?

"Here's one," she said, flashing her phone screen around the table almost too quickly for him to see. From what he'd glimpsed, it looked like a guy in a suit sitting on a park bench sipping an overpriced coffee. *Typical New York.*

"You can hardly even see him he's so far away." Martha clucked her tongue as if she were disappointed. "You must have a better one than that."

"I like this one. He looks so content." She shrugged. "I don't have many pictures of us. When we're together, we're usually too busy doing stuff to stop for a photo op, I guess." Tessa stood from the table, stretching out her long, languid body like a cat waking from a long nap in a sunbeam. "It's been a long day and I'm tired of being interrogated, so if it's all the same to you, I'm going to head to bed early tonight. Which cabin am I staying in this time?"

While Tessa zipped up her boots and grabbed her bag, Martha consulted a piece of paper she'd pulled from her pocket. "The campground was surprisingly booked this week, but I managed to get enough beds for all of us. Looks like you're in cabin thirteen."

"Great. I'll see you in the morning." Tessa disappeared out the door without another glance back.

Logan savored the rest of his dessert then enjoyed a coffee and a game of poker with Travis. When he'd sufficiently kicked his buddy's ass at cards, he figured it was a good time to call it a night. The day had been long and grueling and he still needed to write down the ideas for new physical education games he'd thought of on the drive. With classes starting in less than two weeks, the pressure was weighing heavily on his shoulders. He needed to do well if he hoped to turn his term teaching position into a full-time one until he could find a way to open a new gym. Without this new start in Cutter's Creek, he had nothing—no job, no family, and no life to go back to in New York.

His personal training studio in New York had been a dream come true, one he'd worked hard for, but rent was high and competition was too stiff. He hadn't been able to find clients when the big brand name gyms offered so much more than he could. With his savings depleted, he'd had no choice but to close up shop and fall back on his teaching degree. Luckily Travis had been able to call in a favor and get him a temporary position as the elementary school gym teacher.

He might've earned his teaching degree, but he'd never imagined himself doing it forever.

Someday soon he'd love to open another training studio. Maybe even right in Cutter's Creek where there was no big competition and where the people might actually care about him enough to see his business succeed. Settling down and creating a real life someplace where people knew his name wasn't too much to ask, was it?

"I'm heading to bed for the night. Martha, where do you

have me bunking?"

She consulted her list again then smiled and handed him a key. "It's the first one down the path on the left. Sleep well, dear."

He yawned deeper with each few steps. He was so tired after his long day meeting the rest of Travis's family and…and everything with Tessa. *So much for working on lesson plans tonight.* Inside, the cabin was small and cozy with two single beds and a bathroom and not much else. One bed looked claimed already with the blanket pulled back and bags resting on top of the dresser next to it. He put his things next to the other and was in the process of taking off his shirt when the bathroom door opened.

"Why are you getting naked in my cabin?"

He didn't have to turn around and see the face to recognize the voice—Tessa.

Chapter Three

Tessa stopped in the doorway at the sight of Logan's bare back. That was not what she expected to see when she opened the bathroom door. When she'd gone into the bathroom to get cleaned up and ready for bed, the cabin had been empty, but now…

Now she was staring at Logan, half naked. He turned to face her, and her gaze fell to his sculpted chest. Most guys she'd dated in the past had a decent thing going on. They'd had healthy physiques, not too muscular, not too flabby, and she'd been completely content with that.

After all, she wasn't a world-class supermodel or anything herself. Not that she minded how she looked. In fact, she was happy with herself, extra padding around the edges and all. She was a healthy weight and didn't feel the need to be a stick figure. But Logan Ridley…well, he was a different species altogether.

His clothing had done a fine job of hiding the treasure beneath his shirt. He'd looked of average build before, but now, seeing him in the flesh—heat flared in her cheeks, hotter with every passing second—he was far more than average. He could easily be a bodybuilder if he wasn't already. She'd never actually seen six-pack abs in real life before, only on TV and in magazines of unrealistic celebrity man-candy. Until tonight.

Logan had a perfect set of washboard abs and pecs that made her want to reach out and touch them. She wasn't usually one to put much stock in how someone looked, but…

Damn, he's hot.

But I have a boyfriend—fake boyfriend—and getting through this weekend without anyone finding out Richard isn't real is more important than enjoying the hunkfest in front of me.

If anyone found out the truth, her family would be unrelenting about her moving home. A serious relationship in the city was her safety net to help keep her there—her logical reason for not moving back.

Feeling as if she were about to drool at any second, she snapped her mouth shut, pulled her lips into a cheery smile, and hoped he didn't notice her eyeing him like a life-sized ice cream she wanted to lick from the tip of the cone to the sprinkles on top.

"Apparently, this is my cabin too," he said, finally answering the question. It felt like hours ago that she'd asked what he was doing getting naked in her cabin when it had surely only been seconds. Time had simply stood still while she'd ogled him inappropriately.

"How do you figure that?"

"Because this is where your mom told me I was sleeping for the next week and since she's the boss around here, I didn't think it would be polite to argue. You don't have a problem sleeping with me, do you?"

She swallowed hard as her mind went to naughty places. Her mind definitely wasn't allowed to go to any of those places with Logan. "If by sleeping with you, you mean sharing a cabin, then nope."

He arched his eyebrow. "What else would I mean?"

Oh no, she wasn't going there. She had a fake boyfriend to think about and even if she admitted she didn't have one, she had no intention of hooking up with anyone even remotely connected to Cutter's Creek.

"Just making sure we're on the same page. That's all." She cleared her throat and climbed into bed, which happened to be too close to Logan's.

Logan wandered into the bathroom, leaving the door open while his brushed his teeth.

"I never got a chance to ask you before, but how do you know Travis?" she asked as he walked back into the bedroom. "You didn't grow up here. If you did, I'd remember you."

Only because everyone in town knew everyone else, and not because his muscles and cute smile made him unforgettable.

"I grew up in Manhattan and met Travis at NYU. We were in the same intro classes in our first year. We've been friends ever since."

"How did you end up here camping with us? I was under the impression this was a family camping trip." She pulled her hair up into a twist on top of her head, hoping it didn't look too stupid, not that she was trying to impress Logan or anything, but she didn't want to look like an idiot in front of him either. She couldn't sleep with her hair down while camping. *What if a spider crawled in it?* She shivered at the thought and snuggled down into bed, pulling her blankets up to her chest, and then grabbed her book from the nightstand. Now she'd have to read to take her mind off the idea of spiders anywhere within a five-foot radius of her.

"I'm new to town and don't know anyone other than Travis. I guess they took pity on me being bored until work starts in a few weeks."

"Wait, you moved here? Why would you do that? Why would anyone do that?"

"It's a nice town. I don't know why you wouldn't want to live here. Everyone is friendly and kind and they invite you camping so you feel welcome and included." He shrugged and dropped his pants to the floor, standing in only his boxer-briefs.

She opened her book to a random page and pretended to be completely ignorant of the almost-naked man standing a mere ten feet from her.

Her breathing hitched as she peered over the top of the pages, praying he couldn't see her bite her lip while taking in the bedroom scenery.

Now that's a sizeable package.

Was he actually sharing a room with her and only wearing boxers to bed? Did she really mind that much?

He climbed into bed and her gaze roamed up his body until she got to his face again. When she did, she found him staring at her, accusation and amusement written all over his expression. "Everything all right over there? You got awfully quiet."

"Yeah, sure, fine. Everything is fine. I was just…thinking… about what you were saying." She put down her book on her lap and folded her hands as if she were in the middle of an important business meeting. "The people in town are some of the best you'll ever meet, but a word of advice: There is no privacy here. So if you don't want the whole town to know your business, don't share it with anyone. I'm sure by Monday morning everyone will know we shared this cabin alone tonight."

"And that would be scandalous for you?"

"Wouldn't it be for you, the guy who just moved here?"

"No. I'm okay with my choices and I'm not afraid to let people know who I am. I like that everyone has been so nice and actually wants to meet me. Did you know I got two lasagnas and four trays of cookies delivered the day I moved into my apartment? Can't say that has ever happened in New York, not unless you count the time someone delivered my neighbor's cookies to my door by accident. But I don't think those were regular cookies. He seemed eager to get them back, and his apartment always smelled like a concert venue. After years in the same place, I never even knew my neighbors' names."

"Let's hope the stuff you got this time didn't include any extra mystery ingredients. I can't even imagine those little old ladies all hopped up on stoner cookies." She laughed at the thought. There was no way that would ever happen here. Nothing ever happened here. It was as straight-laced and boring as it could possibly be. "Although, if you got anything from Mrs. Newman, I'd be wary of eating it. She hasn't been all there for a few years now. The last time I ate one of her bake sale cakes I found a cat toy in it."

"Noted. I'll watch out for her."

"What brought you to town anyway? It's not exactly a hub for single guys. I mean, not that your relationship status has anything to do with it, but it's not a lively town to move to."

"I'm here for a maternity leave."

She couldn't hold back her giggle. "I didn't realize you were expecting. When are you due?"

He rolled onto his side, propping himself up on one elbow. "Funny. I'm filling in for a teacher who's taking her maternity leave. You're looking at Cutter's Creek Elementary's newest gym teacher. Pretty exciting, right?"

"Very."

"I know it doesn't sound like much, but it's a stepping stone. Travis got my foot in the door, and it was either accept the position or be out of a job and living in a super expensive city. So here I am."

She yawned, unable to hold back the tiredness creeping into her brain. "Well, I hope you're happier here than I was."

"Not that it's any of my business, but why weren't you happy?"

"Because I'm the wild, rebellious one, remember?" She flipped off her bedside lamp and set her book aside. "I'm sorry, but I'm beat. Between the accident and that last glass of wine you poured me, I'm about to fall asleep talking."

He rolled over and shut off his light too, then settled himself into bed as it creaked and groaned beneath him. These rustic wooden frames probably weren't prepared for the onslaught of muscle they now had to support.

Enough already. So he's hot. And nice, when he's not behind the wheel. Get over it.

A twinkling of moonlight filtered in through the window shades. Nighttime critters seemed to get louder in the darkness, but that didn't stop her from being hyper-aware of Logan's subtle movements in the bed next to hers. Every time he shifted she heard the covers slide against his skin.

What would it feel like to be that blanket?

His voice drifted through the darkness pulling her from her thoughts. "I know you're tired, but since you seemed to have settled in okay with me here, does that mean you're not holding the accident against me anymore?"

"Well, we are stuck rooming together, so we may as well make the best of it, right?" Better to let it go and try to enjoy the week as much as she could.

"I'm glad to hear that. I think it'll be a fun vacation, even if we did get off to a rough start." He yawned loudly and the bed creaked again as he got comfortable. "Goodnight, Tessa. Thanks for the most interesting day I've had in a long time."

"Here's hoping for an uneventful week. Or one filled with copious amounts of alcohol. And yes, I do still blame you for the accident since it was your fault. 'Nite, Logan."

She didn't miss the sound of his deeply annoyed sigh as she fell asleep with a grin on her face.

L ogan groaned and pulled the blanket over his head. The sunlight was bright and it had to be way too early for anyone to be awake. He felt as if he'd slept for minutes not hours. Maybe if he tried harder, he'd be able to fall back asleep until lunch. Surely no one would miss him before that. Except that he could hear the sound of running water somewhere close by. It couldn't be raining with the amount of sun brightening his closed eyelids, which meant it could only be one thing—Tessa in the shower.

Naked Tessa in the shower. Getting soapy. Skin turning pink with the heat from the water.

He groaned again and sat up in bed, adjusting his blanket so it hid his growing arousal. He didn't want to be so turned on by thoughts of Tessa. Nothing good would come of that. Ever. She had a boyfriend. They lived in different places. End of story.

A cheerful tune seeped out from under the bathroom door with the steam, and he could picture her lathering up her body while singing a song currently playing way too often on the top forty.

Stop thinking about her. The ache in his dick doubled. If he didn't get his mind on something else soon, he'd end up easing his pain later in the shower with a soapy lather of his own. It would be better than a raging case of blue balls at least. Just then the singing turned into something resembling more of a wail.

Yikes. She cannot hit those high notes.

A clatter that sounded like metal hitting tiles joined a

wail that had rapidly turned into an ultra-sonic shriek, which could probably be heard in the main cabin. A string of curse words burst forth from the bathroom as Tessa charged into the room, a towel hanging vertically in front of her.

He jumped up from the bed, nearly falling while disentangling himself from the blanket. Tessa slammed into him as he found his balance.

"Spider! Get it off of me!" Her eyes were filled with pure panic and her voice shook as if she were on the verge of tears.

"Where? I don't see anything," he said, gripping her shoulders.

"My hair!" She shrieked so loudly he squinted as if it would help block the sound shooting at him. How did she make such a loud noise?

"Okay, don't panic."

"Don't panic? Are you fucking kidding me? There was a *spider*. Showering with *me*."

He leaned forward and surveyed the situation. He still didn't see anything even close to resembling a spider on her head. She trembled beneath his fingers, but he wasn't sure if it was from fear or the cold air hitting her wet body. Either way, he felt the overwhelming desire to wrap his arms around her, snuggle her against his chest, and make her warm.

She yelled again, this time so close to his ear he feared the subsequent ringing would never stop. "It's on my back! Get it, get it, get it!"

Tessa spun in front of him and he instantly spotted a surprisingly large spider slowly sliding down a river of suds between her shoulder blades headed toward the luscious mounds of her ivory ass. Could he pretend not to have seen it right away so he'd have an excuse to examine her backside longer?

As tempting as it was, he swatted the spider and watched as it hit the wall beside his bed, fell to the floor, and scurried away. If it hadn't been for the distraction of Tessa's naked, soapy flesh beneath his fingertips, he might have been concerned about chasing the spider to kill it. Today the spider could live.

No way was he moving a single muscle from his current position until he absolutely had to. Without thinking, he gripped her hips in his hands. They slid on her wet skin and he squeezed his fingers tighter to hold them still. Her silky flesh was warm and soft, and he longed to feel the curves of her ass pressing against the ache growing even more pronounced in his boxers.

"Did you get it?" she asked, her voice wavering as she peeked over her shoulder.

He had trouble finding his voice. "Yeah. I got it."

She opened her lips as if to say something else. Maybe she did. All he heard was her shaky inhalation of breath as her tongue grazed the edge of her top teeth. The tiny movement inside her mouth was unbelievably erotic.

She sagged against his chest, her head resting on his shoulder and he felt her take a deep breath into her lungs. Then she sighed. "Thank God."

Even as the tension left her body, she still shook, her warm, wet skin gently vibrating against his chest. Despite his willpower, he felt his dick twitch near her lower back and his hands slipped lower on her hips. Goddamn, she felt good. Her body went ramrod straight and she twisted around to face him. As she did, his hand swept across her naked ass, and he nearly moaned with the lightning bolts that shot to his groin. In an instant, she backed away from him and toward the bathroom, her brow furrowed and her index finger trapped between her teeth as if she were trying to solve a complex math problem without a calculator.

Holy shit, he'd give his left nut to be her fingertip right now...to feel her lips surround him, her tongue dancing across his skin. Instead, he was left standing in the middle of a soapy puddle, his heart racing, and his dick straining for release from its confines.

"Thanks for getting the spider. I'm going to rinse off now."

"Want me to supervise in case there are other unwanted guests?" The words were out before he could censor himself. It wasn't his style to be so obviously interested, but it wasn't every morning he found a wet, naked woman in his arms either.

"No, but thanks. I'll use the sink instead. I'm almost done anyway."

She disappeared behind the bathroom door, and he heard the shower turn off then the sink turn on. An image of her bending over the vanity, bare ass on display, flashed through his mind causing the remaining blood in his brain to rush to another area of his anatomy. He perched on the edge of his bed, resting his head in his hands for a minute before scanning the floorboards for any sign of that spider. He saw nothing.

Logan wasn't a big fan of creepy-crawly things either, but he was willing to wake up early every morning for the next week so he could find a new eight-legged friend to take up residence in their shower. Anything to get Tessa naked and in his arms again.

Chapter Four

Tessa paused for one last deep breath before opening the bathroom door while praying she was ready to face Logan. She hadn't been able to convince herself to finish showering after the spider incident, so she'd settled for rinsing the shampoo out of her hair in the sink. Tomorrow, when she'd had a little time and distance to forget about the eight legs sharing her water, she'd face her fear and shower again. Until then, that entire area was the enemy, and she was smart enough not to cross into its territory. After dressing, blow-drying, styling, and applying makeup, she could find no other ways to delay the inevitable. The sooner she confronted the awkward situation that had occurred, the better.

He'd seen her freak out over a spider. Anyone would act the same in her position.

He'd seen her half naked, big deal. It was just a little skin.

He'd touched her bare ass with his large, strong, spider-hunting hand. Just another day at the cabin, right? If you bunk together, sooner or later someone's bound to see some intimate skin.

Pulling open the door, she found the cabin empty and she sagged against the doorframe with relief. Thank God she wouldn't have to deal with him yet. A few extra minutes to strengthen her backbone would make it easier. Of course, not running into him here meant she'd inevitably have to run into him around her family and that would make the situation infinitely more awkward. Unless he was a smart man and didn't mention the spider incident when anyone else was around.

Slipping into her sneakers, she jogged over to the main cabin. It might be summer, but in the mountains, the mornings and evenings were cool. The spaghetti strap tank top she wore would be perfect for later, but even with the light sweater over top, she was chilly this morning and jogging warmed her up.

Oh, who am I kidding. Jogging sucks, but spiders suck worse. Jogging to the cabin was the fastest way to get from point A to point B without a spider jumping, climbing, or creeping on her again. Once per day was more than enough.

The scent of freshly brewed coffee and her mom's warm cinnamon buns greeted her like a lover's kiss. Not that she was thinking about kissing anyone, but if she were thinking about kissing someone, it would probably conjure the same response, make her mouth water, and her head spin with desire.

"About time you joined us," her mom said, handing her a pastry on a plate and a mug of coffee—light and sweet, just how she liked it.

She took a seat at the other end of the table from Logan and tried not to look directly at him. She didn't want to know if this morning's adventure was still lingering in his mind as well. Better not to know.

"Sorry, I didn't realize you were waiting on me," she said after sipping her coffee.

"I wondered where you'd gotten to, that's all. Thought

maybe something had delayed you this morning since I know you tend to be an early riser. But then Logan wandered over for breakfast so…"

So what exactly?

"It took me an extra few minutes to get cleaned up today, that's all. I'll try to be quicker tomorrow."

"We want to spend as much time with you as we can, Tessa-bear," her mom cooed. "We only get you home for the week, you know."

"Since I'm the one you're referring to, yes, I'm aware of my scheduled return back to the city." *And I won't let anyone stop me from leaving.*

Her mom sighed and turned back toward the counter. Tessa sighed too, feeling guilt settle into her stomach because of her grouchy comment. It wasn't a feeling she'd missed while being away. She didn't mean to be a bitch to her mom or anyone else. She simply didn't want to be hounded anymore about where she lived.

She licked sticky cinnamon bun frosting from her fingers.

Glancing up from her plate, her gaze landed on Logan who was holding his coffee cup near his lips yet wasn't actually taking a sip. His tongue swiped across his lower lip seconds after hers did the same, a mirror image.

This morning, she'd turned in his arms and that mouth of his had been close to her own. So close it made her want to taste him. *Too* close if she wanted her fake boyfriend to stick around for a while, which she did. Leaving would be even harder if she didn't have someone important to go back to the city for, at least as far as everyone else was concerned.

Nope. She couldn't think about how tempting Logan's mouth had been earlier or how much more tempting it was now that he would taste of sweet pastry and strong coffee— two of her favorite things. Logan was a complicating factor she didn't need.

"No reason to get grouchy, Tessa-bear. That racket we heard coming from your cabin must have been you waking up on the wrong side of the bed."

She stared at her mother. "You heard me screaming, while I was in a cabin *alone* with a man I barely know and shouldn't even be rooming with, and you didn't bother to wander over to find out if I was okay?"

"Well, we didn't think it was anything to make a big deal over," Sally said with a shrug from her place on the couch where she nursed her coffee.

"Your sister screaming isn't a big deal?"

Mary rolled her eyes. "It's not like you were being murdered in there or anything. Relax. Drink your caffeine fix. You need it."

"How did you know I wasn't being murdered? No one even checked on me," she said feeling flustered. Didn't they understand at all why she was concerned? What if it had been a weirdo psychopath in her cabin this morning instead of a spider?

"We didn't want to interrupt anything that might've been going on between you two. That's all." Her mother clucked her tongue as she meandered back into the kitchen as if the conversation were nothing.

"What would we have been doing that would lead to screaming?" she asked.

Travis and Sally glanced toward each other grinning. "It's more about *how* you do it than *what* you do," Travis said.

He didn't imply…

"I wouldn't… We just met…" Her cheeks grew hot, and it had nothing to do with the steaming cup of coffee she hugged in her palms. "There was a spider in the shower. I freaked out. That's why I was screaming."

"I saved her," Logan said.

"He saved you in the shower?" Mary asked, wide-eyed.

"Nice going, bro," Travis said, holding up his coffee like a salute of manly solidarity.

Logan smirked but didn't correct her brother-in-law's inaccurate assumption.

"He wasn't in the shower with me," she said, her voice imploring them to get their imaginations out of the gutter, or out of the shower with her and Logan.

"It's okay if you want to admit to being a little freaky. Mom's in the kitchen and can't hear us anyways." Travis winked.

"We weren't in the shower together getting freaky. We only met yesterday. What kind of a girl do you think I am?"

"Now that you're not around, we don't know anymore. Maybe the big city changed you into some kind of sexual misfit."

"First of all, showering with someone else doesn't make you a sexual misfit. It makes you environmentally conscious." The room around her laughed and she felt her blood pressure boiling as she attempted to ignore them and maintain control in her voice. "And secondly, if the big city has changed me, it has opened my eyes to how much more world there is outside of this backwoods little town you think is the center of the universe."

She pushed away from the table. "From now on, nothing that happens in our cabin is any of your business, not that anything else is going to happen… Or did happen." Grabbing her cup, Tessa was about to leave to finish her coffee outside in the peace and quiet—God help the spider who bothered her right now!—when her mother walked into the room.

"I do hope you two won't find the place too lonely out there, all alone. Every night," she said.

"Why, exactly, am I sharing a cabin with him, Mom? I don't even know him."

Her mother smiled sweetly. "Well, he had to sleep

somewhere, and after all the experiences you've had on your own in the big city and how much you love being surrounded by strangers, we figured you'd be more comfortable rooming with Logan rather than your family. Of course, that was before I knew about that other boyfriend person, but what's done is done." She shrugged as if it was no big deal. "I'm sure you'll be fine. You always are."

Tessa closed her eyes and quickly counted to ten. *I will not let circumstance risk my family finding out the truth about Richard.*

Just because she'd be alone with Logan every night didn't mean she would suddenly fall into his strong arms and snuggle against his gloriously sculpted chest. Nor would she spend each night lying in the dark beside him, talking about their lives and getting to know each other like they had last night, like learning about how he was an elementary school teacher and probably a super nice guy who cared about making kids healthy. No way. Touching and talking were off limits.

In fact, the less time she spent in the cabin alone with him the better. From now on instead of calling it bedtime early each night to avoid hanging out with him and her family, she'd stay up until she was one second from falling asleep in the fire pit and go straight to bed. Alone. To sleep.

She opened her eyes and forced herself to feel centered and completely not bothered. "I'm sure Logan and I will be fine. I'm going to finish my coffee outside." She turned on her heel and resisted the urge to slam the door behind her.

"Why am I so grouchy?" she asked herself out loud as she perched uncomfortably on the edge of a picnic table by the lake, not too far from the cabin. "Why can't I ignore their comments?"

"I've been wondering that myself," Logan said sitting down beside her, close enough that their thighs brushed against one another.

"It's a rhetorical question and one not meant for anyone else's ears," she said.

"Well then, you shouldn't have spoken it out loud. That's what internal thoughts are for."

She didn't need him telling her anything about internal thoughts. She'd had plenty of those lately too and most had been sexy and about the man confronting her. Anytime those wanted to stop intruding on her normal thoughts would be great. "I didn't know anyone followed me since I came out here to be alone."

He continued as if he hadn't heard her and he obviously couldn't take a hint. "I haven't known you for long, and I've only known your family for a few weeks, not including Travis, but it seems like you get annoyed in a nanosecond where they're concerned. As an outsider looking in, it seems a little uncalled for. And I won't mention how you've seemed to be mad at me pretty much constantly since we met."

"You're suddenly an expert on my feelings and my family? You think you know what I should feel?" She couldn't help defending herself even though she knew everything he said was true.

"It seems like you're tense, that's all. If you want someone to talk to about it, someone impartial, I'm here."

That wasn't what she expected. Guys didn't usually want to sit around talking about feelings, theirs or anyone else's. "Thanks," she mumbled. "I think I'm a little on edge being home. No one wanted me to leave and it's the first time I've been back. I knew they would hint about wanting me to stay but I didn't think they'd be so blatantly intrusive about it."

"What's so wrong with Cutter's Creek?" he asked, his voice quiet and comforting, not demanding and defensive like her family's would be if asking the same thing.

"Everything. Nothing."

"Well that clears it up." He chuckled and nudged her

shoulder with his.

"It's…" How could she put into words all her feelings about this place to a guy who'd only been around a couple of weeks and who seemed to like it? She couldn't and even if she could, she wasn't sure she wanted to. Some things were better kept to herself. "It's not the place for me."

"But New York City is?"

"Yeah. For now at least."

They were silent for a few minutes. While she finished her coffee, they watched as geese landed on the surface of the lake, coming and going as a group. Always as a group. *What if one wants to fly off on its own to explore for a while? Do all the others have to go too?*

"I think I know exactly what you need to improve your mood," he said suddenly standing up.

There's a therapist in every group, she thought bitterly. *Exactly what I need, more advice about how to live my life and what choices to make.*

"Oh? What's that?" Her attempt to rein in the bitchiness was futile.

He ignored her, his smile remaining intact. "The best thing you could do is come for a jog around the lake. It'll do you good to get moving, and the fresh air always helps clear my mind and refocus my thoughts. When we're back, I'll make you one of my famous green smoothies if I can find a blender in the kitchen. How's that sound?"

"Like a heart attack followed by an overly strong gag reflex." The thought of a green smoothie made her shiver. She'd done the juice cleanse thing her first month in the city since everywhere she went someone was on one and saying how wonderful it was. Three days in and the mere thought of the green juice made her gag. The juice cleanse had been a mistake, and she wouldn't willingly make it again with Logan or his famous smoothie. "Thanks, but I'll pass."

"Are you sure? It might help with your outlook on life. It couldn't hurt at least."

Her outlook wasn't bad most days. Being home and feeling the pressure to move back did something to her, changed her in some way. Not a way she liked either.

"I think I hear another cup of coffee calling my name. I'll see you when you get back," she said, hopping off the table to head into the cabin for a refill. *That didn't sound too eager or anything, did it?* That wasn't the impression she wanted to leave him with. "Or not, whatever. Have a good jog."

He finished stretching quickly then turned and jogged up to the lake, following the edge of the water around a bend and into the woods where she couldn't see him, but not quick enough for her to miss the strength in his legs as he pushed off the soft ground, propelling himself forward.

It was one of the many things she shouldn't notice when it came to Logan, along with his easy-going personality, his witty sense of humor that matched hers, and that he was a guy who she barely knew but who was willing to come out here and check on her, even if it meant talking about her feelings. What guys did that? Nice guys like Logan, apparently.

Now if only she could find a guy like him in the city, she'd be set and wouldn't need to make up a boyfriend ever again. Then convincing her family her new life was not in Cutter's Creek wouldn't be so hard, because it would be true.

As it was right now, she felt like she was lying about every aspect of her life—she didn't have a boyfriend, she wanted to be happy but wasn't sure she could honestly claim that status, and her big painting career had started out with her painting window murals on coffee shops and retail stores, instead of canvasses hanging in galleries. Definitely not the way she'd seen things working out. She wanted to claim everything was wonderful, but she couldn't because everything was more challenging than she expected. Nothing seemed to be falling into place like she'd imagined it would. Nope, but she couldn't admit any of that to her family.

More time, that's all she needed. With enough hard work and perseverance, she'd get exactly where she wanted to be. In the city she was a nobody, anonymous, like she'd always wanted, and it would take a little more time for people to learn about her and her work. But they would learn about her eventually, and once they did, there'd be no stopping her dreams.

The same couldn't be said if she moved back to Cutter's Creek. Sure, here everyone knew her name, but no one cared about her dreams.

Chapter Five

Logan found a smooth branch thick enough to support his weight but still thin enough to wrap his hands around, then proceeded to do fifty pull-ups in quick succession. His jog around the lake had been a good workout given the uneven terrain and the rise and fall in elevation. The muscles up and down his legs ached, unaccustomed to running on uneven ground like this. His body was still used to pounding the pavement of city paths.

Even with the aching muscles, he still much preferred this run to his usual ones. Soft trails beat hard pavement any day, both in workout intensity and benefits to his body. Clean mountain air didn't compare to city pollution. And there wasn't even a tiny piece of him that missed the honking of car horns or rattle of buses and trains when he could hear birds chirping, squirrels scampering, and leaves crunching underfoot.

This was the life he was meant to live. Now he had to figure out a way to hold on to it.

Ideally, he'd be able to open a new personal training studio where he could give classes and private one-on-one coaching on a daily basis like he did in the city. Only here, he might stand a chance of paying the rent. With no big competitive gyms in the area, he would definitely have the market share.

He dropped to the ground and did one hundred pushups before standing and shaking out his arms. That would have to be good enough for today. Otherwise, he'd run the risk of missing out on other activities with the Cutters and he didn't want that to happen. It was nice of them to invite him out for a family trip. Having the town's founding family on his side would make it slightly easier for the other town's people to accept him too, since he'd heard from Travis that some of them could be hesitant to welcome newcomers.

Finding the cabin empty, he quickly showered and changed and was ready for the rest of the day in less than fifteen minutes. On his way back to the main cabin, he saw Travis headed toward one of the pickup trucks.

"Where are you off to?" he asked, walking up to the driver's side door.

"Martha wants a bonfire tonight and there's barely enough wood for the fireplace, so she's sending me out to get some. Want to come for the ride?"

"Sure. I've got nowhere else to be."

Logan hopped into the passenger seat and bounced around as Travis drove over the rough ground that made up the driveway. "How come we're not chopping down a tree outside of the cabin?"

Travis laughed. "You serious?"

Logan sighed. Apparently he'd said something stupid. If he wasn't such a city boy, maybe he'd have an inkling of an idea about what he'd said wrong. "I guess not."

"Sorry, man. Sometimes I forget how different it is to grow up in the city instead of somewhere rural."

"Wish I could forget," he muttered under his breath.

He didn't want to be an outsider anymore. The whole time he lived in Manhattan he'd yearned for open spaces, the big outdoors, and a place where someone might actually care about him enough to learn his name and say hi. Now that he had a shot at getting that life, he couldn't figure out how to fit in. Who knew it would be so damn hard?

"I didn't mean anything by it. I forgot you don't know this stuff yet. No worries. We can't cut down the trees around the cabin because if everyone did that, then we'd be camping in a pasture and not in a forest."

Logical. I'm a moron.

"Even if we could cut down one of our trees, we'd have to season the wood, meaning we'd have to leave it out to dry for a long time. If you try to burn wood right after you cut it, you end up with a lot of smoke."

"Good to know. I guess I have a lot to learn about living here."

"You don't have to know everything. People here are used to doing things the right way without asking. Pay attention and you'll catch on quick."

"And if I don't? What if I'm destined to be a city boy forever?" Logan asked. His voice held the tone of a joke, but he was serious.

"Then we'll have to run you out of town with pitchforks, of course." Travis laughed before reaching over and punching him in the shoulder. "Relax. No one is that high-strung here. I managed to weasel my way in and you will too."

"Yeah, but were already used to small-town life, and you married a Cutter. That automatically makes you a member of the founding family of Cutter's Creek. You got a ticket on the easy train. Somehow, I don't think it'll go quite so well for me."

"You never know."

"Yeah, how do you figure that?" he asked.

"There's still a couple of Cutter daughters who are unattached, and at least one of them thinks you're hot stuff."

There was no doubt Travis was referring to Tessa since Mary had barely given him a once over since he met her. She definitely wasn't interested in anything more than being friendly with her brother-in-law's friend.

Tessa on the other hand... At times she'd looked at him as if she were imagining touching every square inch of his body. With her tongue. The thought of her touching him, licking him, made his cargo shorts tight. Other times, she seemed surprised by something he'd said as if she thought he was another meathead without a decent thought in his brain. He was used to that stereotype and it was especially amusing when he got to crush it by showing his strength in smarts as well as muscle.

Then there were all those times she looked like she was one second away from tearing a strip off him with her words, her anger spiking hot and fast. He might actually enjoy those moments the most. When she got fired up about something, her eyes sparkled and her body quivered slightly as if she were holding back a ton of pent up energy. Every time he'd seen that happen, he'd wondered what it would be like if she directed that energy at something else, like his body. Maybe she'd rip his clothes to shreds as she tore them off, then mounted him like he was a prize-winning stallion.

A guy could dream.

Regardless, she'd made it clear that she had a boyfriend and that's all there was to it.

"If you're talking about Mary, I think you're delusional. She couldn't be less interested in me. And if you're talking about Tessa, well then, you're forgetting her 'super serious' boyfriend in the city."

"That didn't sound jealous at all," Travis said. He pulled the vehicle into a parking lot at the campground store and hopped out before Logan could defend himself. He wasn't jealous of Richard "the Dick" stroker.

He hopped out of the truck and leaned against it while he waited for Travis to pay, then they loaded up the truck with bundles of wood and jumped back inside.

"I am not," Logan said, hating that his tone made him sound defensive and thereby guilty.

"You aren't what? Hot for my sister-in-law? Yeah, sure, right."

"And what's that supposed to mean?"

"It means I've known you long enough to recognize that look in your eyes."

"What look? There's no look in my eyes. I don't know what you're talking about."

"That glint you get when you see something you like, *someone* you like. That gleam that always precedes you putting all of your energy into getting what you want." Travis sounded so matter of fact it pissed Logan off.

He did not get a look in his eye over a girl, any girl. Not a gleam and certainly not a fucking glint. And he most certainly didn't get that way over Tessa, Tessa who had a boyfriend and an attitude the size of Canada.

"Have you forgotten she hates me since I 'almost killed her and ran her off a mountain' the other day?"

"She was grouchy, wasn't she?"

"You could say that."

"Well, I don't think she still feels that way. I can tell. She's over it. But…"

"But what?" Logan gazed out the window at the passing trees so that hopefully his friend wouldn't know how much this conversation was getting to him.

"She might be over the accident, but I'm not so sure she's over you."

What did that mean? Did he see something in Tessa that

Logan didn't? Something that would lead him to believe she might be into him. Did he want her to be into him?

He stayed quiet the rest of the ride back to the cabin. As they pulled in, Tessa and Mary walked across the yard to a supply shed and grabbed a couple of long oars. The fact that she was currently in a bikini—skimpier than he would have thought was her taste, bright blue like the sky on a clear summer day, and so sexy he imagined taking it off with his teeth—was of little concern.

He hopped out of the truck and began unloading wood. Pain shot through his foot as he unsuccessfully dropped a heavy bundle, missing the pile completely. He barely held back a string of profanities, not wanting the other Cutters to overhear him in case they weren't the kind to do that sort of thing.

"Smooth, bro. Real smooth." Travis laughed and grabbed another couple of bundles out of the truck, tossing them to the side of the cabin with ease. "Just because you're trying to avoid looking at Tessa doesn't mean she's avoiding you."

Logan glanced around in what he hoped was a casual way only to find Tessa eyeing him as he tossed firewood alongside Travis. He flexed more than he needed to while grabbing another bundle of wood, and he didn't miss when she bit her bottom lip as if she were holding back a sigh. Now he saw what Travis was talking about. She did an awful lot of looking for a girl who was happily involved with the man of her dreams already.

Suddenly her gaze met his and her expression turned startled, like a peeping Tom caught peering in a bedroom window. Whipping her head away from him, she bolted toward the lake.

Interesting.

Tessa shook her head then ran to catch up to Mary at the water's edge. She hadn't noticed Mary wasn't at her side anymore when she'd stopped at the sight of Travis and Logan unloading firewood. His thick arms flexed with the weight of the wood as he tossed the bundles with ease, like coins into a fountain. Then his gaze had locked with hers and she'd suddenly realized not only was she alone, but also staring at Logan in a way that was all too suggestive. Damn it, she'd even been biting her lip to hold back a groan of pleasure. Men as hot as Logan should not exist outside of movies and romance novels.

"Sorry about that. I, uh, tripped over a log and had to stop for a second." Her excuse was lame but all she could think of with her cloudy brain.

"Tripped over Logan's big arms is more like it."

"That's not even possible. He was unloading the firewood with Travis. Not that I noticed what he was doing or anything." She snapped her mouth shut. A woman with a serious boyfriend did not ogle other men.

"Sure. Whatever you say." Mary took a squirt of sunscreen from the bottle then handed it to Tessa. "Better cover up good before we go out. The sun will be hot reflecting off the water."

"True. It's beautiful out there. I can't wait to be in the middle of the lake surrounded by nothing but peace and quiet."

"Sounds like heaven to me," Logan said, walking up behind the girls. "Want me to get that spot between your shoulder blades. I can tell you missed it with the lotion."

Why did he have to come over here? Couldn't she have two minutes without him in her space?

"I got it, thanks."

"Actually, you don't got it, but if you want to burn, that's cool too. Your call," he said, nonchalantly, spreading lotion up his arm to his shoulder. He worked the sunscreen in quickly then pulled off his shirt and started applying it to his chest.

Hot. Damn. His chest was even better when a spider wasn't threatening her life. She turned away. "Mary, can you get that spot on my back for me?"

"I'm in the middle of doing my legs. Give me a few minutes, okay?"

The sound of lotion squirting out of the bottle behind her made her turn back to face Logan. He smiled. "I promise I'll be gentle. Besides, if I do yours, then you can do mine."

"I don't think that's appropriate since I have a boyfriend and all."

"You didn't think it was inappropriate when there was a spider crawling down your back." He winked as if remembering the moment in detail.

He probably was. She was. Every single moment of being almost naked with him was burned into her memory, and she couldn't count the number of times she'd already replayed the scene in her head.

"He probably wouldn't like you touching me," she said. That sounded legit.

"So he'd prefer you get a sunburn?"

At least she had bottoms on this time, and she didn't want to get sunburnt, which she was likely to on the best days. Being on the water for an hour would make it even more probable. "Fine. Thank you for offering."

Pulling her hair over her shoulder, she turned away. The second his hands touched her, her eyelids fluttered closed and she sighed. Damn, his hands felt good on her body. Firm and strong, yet his caress was so gentle it almost tickled. When his fingers slipped underneath the bow tied against her spine, her knees weakened.

"That should do it. Can you do me now?" He chuckled. "I mean, can you put lotion on my back?"

Why don't we buy spray lotion? She put a dollop of lotion

in her hand and rubbed her palms together, then paused before placing them on his back. *You can do it. It's only lotion.* Simply one human helping another human so they don't crisp in the sun. *Heaven help me.* She sighed and bit her lip.

His skin was already warmed from the sun. Smooth and supple. As she massaged in the creamy lotion, there was no ignoring the tingles of electricity sparking in her fingertips and running straight to her girly bits. She did not want to feel this way. Not now. Not here. Not with Logan.

Pushing the feeling aside, she quickly rubbed in the remainder of the sunscreen hoping she did it evenly. The last thing she needed was to do a shoddy job and end up having to slather his naked torso with cooling aloe gel tonight.

"You're all done!" she said with a chipper tone as she smacked him on the shoulder playfully.

"Thanks. So what are we doing on the lake today? This is quite the oversized oar you've got here." He handled the wood as if it were a thing of beauty, caressing the smooth surface with his fingertips.

"Jealous?" she asked, smirking.

He arched an eyebrow and she cursed her blunt remark. "Oh, no, sugar. I've got more than enough on my own."

Tessa's pulse pounded and her breath quickened. "I didn't mean…"

Logan shrugged. "You did, but it's okay. I don't mind you questioning as long as you believe my answer. Of course, if you need physical evidence, you let me know, okay?"

She cleared her throat and tried to ignore his comments and how they made her hotter than the sun beating down on her back. "Mary and I were heading out onto the lake."

"Sounds like fun. What do I need?"

He didn't think he was joining them today, did he? "*We're* going paddle boarding. I don't know what *you're* doing so I don't know what you need."

"You apparently lost your manners in the move." Mary slipped off her sandals and stepped to the water's edge. "We have plenty of gear. Go grab yourself a board and an oar from the shed."

"I'll be back in a minute." Logan strode off to the supply shed.

Tessa instantly felt guilt wash over her again at being rude to him, but she couldn't help it. She needed a break. "I thought it was just us today?" Tessa said, her voice bordering on whining. She wanted peace and quiet out on the lake, not Logan and his distracting body.

"It was, but now it's Logan too. And by the look of it" — she motioned to the cabin where the front door was clanking shut behind swimsuit clad Travis and Sally—"they're coming too. This is a family camping trip, Tessa, not a girls weekend. And you shouldn't be so rude to Logan all the time. He's a nice guy who's trying to fit in with the rest of us. How would you feel being on a trip where you only knew one person and someone there refused to accept you?"

Tessa bit her lip and kept her mouth shut. Well, if the tables were turned and she was in Logan's position, she wouldn't like it, that's for sure. "I'll try to be nicer. I didn't mean to make him uncomfortable."

"Besides, if you give him half a chance, you might actually find you like him." Mary stepped onto her paddleboard, found her balance, and shoved off with her oar, drifting out a few feet into the lake.

That's what I'm afraid of.

Chapter Six

Tessa sighed. "Any day, big guy. It's only a little paddleboard."

"I'm coming."

"So is Christmas." She rolled her eyes at herself. *Totally something Dad would say.*

He ignored her and gingerly climbed onto his board, separating his feet in a way that looked uncomfortable and ineffective for balancing on the water.

"If you move your feet so they're parallel under your hips and not forward and back, you'll feel more stable." She offered the suggestion then glanced around the lake. The rest of their group had already paddled off and somehow she'd been left to tend to the newbie. *Lucky me.* "Or you can start out on your knees. That's how they teach kids at the beach."

"I'm not a kid and I'll do it standing up." He shifted his feet cautiously as if he was worried about going in. He should be worried. It was common for beginners to end up in the water at least a couple of times on their first try. "If you can manage it, so can I."

"What's that supposed to mean?"

And Mary said Tessa was the one being rude.

"Well, you don't strike me as the most athletic person in the world." He got his feet into position and slowly stood, arms out to the sides like he was walking a tight rope.

"If you're referring to the extra five pounds on my ass and boobs, you're a dead man. I'll drown you in the lake and claim it was a paddle boarding accident. Think long and hard before you answer."

He gripped his paddle in both hands as his gaze examined her areas in question. "Now I'm only making an educated guess here, since I haven't had any hands-on experience, but as far as I can tell, your ass and boobs are perfect."

By the time he looked her in the eyes again, her entire body felt heated by his gaze. She should've known better than to say something like that. "I have a boyfriend," she blurted out, as much a reminder for herself as for him.

"So you've said. And does he think you have a little extra weight on your ass and boobs? Is that why you're self-conscious about it? 'Cause if that's that case, I'd be happy to tell him what an asshole he is. I'm something of an expert on the human body, at least as far as healthy body weight and exercise is concerned, and I don't see anything wrong with yours."

"No. Rich is fine with it. Me. My boobs." Was she sunburned already because her face felt hot?

"I thought he went by Richard."

Damn it. What difference did it make and why did he remember that? "I call him Rich."

He nodded, looking not at all satisfied with her answer. Too bad. That was the only answer she was giving him. The less she talked about her fake boyfriend, the more likely she'd be able to keep her story straight.

"I guess a finance guy isn't that interested in the human

form. Probably too busy dealing with numbers, right? At least, I think you said he was a finance guy."

"Yep."

"I'm sure that's exciting and important work."

"It is. Are you ready to paddle now?" she asked, moving a little further out on the lake.

He followed closely, seeming to have gotten the hang of the board. "I think you said he works at some office on the Upper East Side, right?"

Did I say that? Or was it the financial district? Or Wall Street specifically?

"Yah-huh." *Agreeable enough yet still non-committal.*

"I think I'm getting it," he said, floating up next to her, then drifting past. "This is pretty easy once you've got the stance right."

Her body relaxed since he wasn't talking about her pretend boyfriend anymore. She'd wanted to come out on the lake to relax, not talk. Gripping her paddle, she worked to catch up. For a guy who'd only just learned to stand on the board a few minutes ago, he was surprisingly fast already. Well, she wouldn't let him be better at this than she was.

She paddled hard and caught up to him, then sailed past him. Glancing over her shoulder, she called, "What were you saying about me not being athletic? Looks like this non-athletic girl left you in the dust. Take that, Mr. Muscles, and your shitty balance."

"You noticed." He smirked and paddled after her, his chest and arms flexing as he did.

How could she not? "Considering you've been shirtless for most of the time I've known you, it's sort of impossible to miss your bulging ego, I mean muscles."

"Noticing bulges too? Interesting."

She whipped around on her board. "That's not what I meant and you know it." How dare he change this around to mean something dirty when all she did was defend her athleticism?

Her foot slipped on the board, and she grabbed for her paddle, hoping it would steady her. Instead, it shifted her balance further, making her foot slide on the slick surface. In one quick swoop, she was in the water sputtering and coughing as she came to the surface, grabbing blindly for her board. When she felt it under her fingertips, she pulled herself up and tried to blink away the water in her eyes.

"Hey!" Logan shouted.

Another splash sounded on the other side of her board. When she wiped her eyes clear of wet hair and water, she found Logan a foot away and soaking wet. "What happened to you?"

"You tipped my board and flipped me. That's what happened." He pushed his wet hair off his forehead, making it stand up in spikes.

"I didn't. I grabbed my board."

"No, you grabbed mine."

She tilted her head, annoyed. "Then where is my board?"

He pointed over her shoulder to where her board was currently floating at least fifty feet away and drifting farther at an alarming rate. Her paddle was headed a completely different direction.

"Shit. I guess I'm going for a swim." She tried to push away from the board but he grabbed her forearm, stopping her. Despite the cold water, his hand was warm.

"Hop on my board and we'll go collect your stuff together."

"I don't need your help. I'm a good swimmer."

"I didn't say you weren't, but why not save your energy for the paddle boarding and hop a ride with me?"

He made a good point. Swimming in the lake was hard and it would tire her out fast. "You're right," she said, meeting his gaze, which was the closest they been to each other since the spider incident.

He chuckled. "Did it hurt a lot to say that?"

She narrowed her eyes. "Shut it. So, how are we doing this? Cling to the side and kick our way to my stuff?"

"I thought more along the lines of we could both sit on it and I could paddle us over. You hop up first."

She followed his command and used her arm strength, or what there was of it, to pull her top half out of the water and onto the board. In turn, she also ended up with her breasts pressed against the surface, making them almost overflow the tiny triangles of her bikini top.

Why didn't I wear the one-piece? Because I wanted the tan.

Quickly, she propped herself up on her elbows. "Should I go the rest of the way or do you want to come part way up first?"

His knuckles looked almost white as he gripped the sides of the board. "You should go all the way."

Did he mean that to sound like a suggestion for something else? Surely not.

Water splashed behind her as she kicked her legs and pulled herself the rest of the way onto the board, straddling it. She'd sat like this hundreds of times before but today this position made her feel vulnerable, almost as if she was on display. She didn't miss his gaze traveling her body once again.

A second later he was up on his knees behind her, wobbling around unsteadily.

"I think you need to sit like me. Otherwise it's way too rocky. If you sit this way, our legs will help keep us level."

"Okay," he said. She felt him settle behind her. "I think you need to come back toward the middle a bit since the front is dipping into the water."

Tessa planted her hands in front of her, then lifted her hips and shifted back a few spots. She stopped, frozen the second she felt his inner thighs on her hips. Now she'd gone too far.

Logan attempted to use the long oar to paddle them toward her gear still floating farther away, but it was bulky and kept hitting their knees.

"Ouch. I'm going to be bruised if we keep this up. Hand me the paddle." Laying it across the front of the board, it easily missed the surface of the water. "Let's use our hands. It's not far."

Leaning forward, she dipped her hands into the water on either side of her legs and scooped it back toward Logan. They glided forward slightly. "This'll work."

Logan joined her and together they coasted forward on the surface of the calm lake, the only sound the lapping of their hands in the water. With every stroke, she felt Logan's chest brush against her back and every time she found herself leaning into him more and more.

His touch was much more comforting than she wanted it to be, more enjoyable than she cared to admit. Every press of his body against hers made her long for another. When they finally reached her paddle, she dragged air into her lungs as if she'd been underwater holding it. True, she was working up a sweat moving this way, but more than that, she was having a hard time resisting the allure of Logan behind her. The thought of him breathing on the back of her neck and rocking his hips into hers stole her breath.

The urge to turn and wrap her legs around his waist almost overwhelmed her. Maybe if she made conversation she'd stop wanting to sit on his lap and get dirty out here on the lake.

"So, where did you teach when you lived in New York?" Not that she'd have any clue where the school was, but she figured it was a safe subject.

"I was a teacher a few years ago. Most recently I had my own personal training studio."

A business owner? Now that she thought about it, she could kind of see it—take charge attitude, confident, not afraid to tell it how he sees it. And if he was a personal trainer then he was also willing to inflict pain and torture all in the name of health. That's why he liked those green smoothies so much. Kale was probably the secret ingredient that made people suddenly want to do handstand pushups. She would never be one of those people.

"What made you leave your business and everything the city has to offer to come here?" No reason was good enough in her mind.

"A fresh start." He sighed and leaned on her a little more, almost as if he sought comfort from her. "My studio struggled with the big brand name gyms to begin with, but when the building manager raised the rent, I couldn't make it anymore. So here I am."

The defeat in his voice was strange since she'd only ever heard him be cheerful and upbeat. This new tone was one she didn't care for. She wasn't into the whole fitness lifestyle herself but that didn't mean she wanted to see him fail at it.

"You think Cutter's Creek will be a better place for you?"

"I'm hopeful it will be. It's the kind of place I want to live and it definitely doesn't hurt that there's not a brand name gym to be seen for fifty miles. I might actually have a shot here."

"If you can get people to workout. People here aren't quite as health-minded as you are."

"We'll see. I can be pretty charming and persuasive when I want to be."

She didn't doubt that. Earlier she'd almost considered joining him on his jog. That was a first. And a last. Jogging did not sound like fun, even with a sweaty beefcake like Logan next to her.

A few more strokes and she'd be back at her own board.

The realization that her ride between Logan's legs was almost over made her long for her board to float farther away. It felt so good to be this close to him. She sagged back against him, her chest heaving with exertion and desire. His chest was hot against her back, a stark contrast to the cold water surrounding them, and she wanted to rest there forever—lay her head back on his shoulders, close her eyes, and soak up some rays.

Logan half sighed, half moaned. The rumble in his chest vibrated against her skin sending little shockwaves through her body. What was she doing and why couldn't she make herself stop? Damn it. She knew better than to get caught up in this moment and yet she leaned into him more. It wasn't good for her health, or her sanity. Or her overactive and underused sex drive.

"If you need to rest and catch your breath here for a few minutes, I don't mind." His words came out as a warm caress on her earlobe and she wanted more than anything to do exactly as he suggested. But she couldn't.

A girl with a boyfriend wouldn't have even leaned against him for a second. There was no way she could linger. "I'm good, thanks. I think I was winded for a second. I'm fine now."

Without waiting for a response, she reluctantly peeled herself away from him and dove into the water. The cold instantly cleared the hazy desire that had clouded her intentions and crumbled her inhibitions, and by the time she popped up onto her board again, she was back to feeling like herself as if cuddling with Logan had never happened.

The fact that her back still tingled from where his pecs pressed against her was nothing more than a figment of her imagination and one she was about to delete from memory.

"Everything okay?" he asked standing up and looking ready to go again as if nothing had transpired between them.

"Yep. I'm ready to head home. I think the sun is stronger

than usual. I'm not really feeling like myself right now."

"I'll come with you. Are you able to paddle back?"

"Totally. No worries. Let's go, okay?"

"Lead the way. I couldn't even guess which way the cabin is now. I'm not even sure which way we came from. Nothing on shore looks familiar."

As Tessa headed toward shore, she gave herself an internal pep talk with every stroke of the paddle.

You will not look at Logan's deliciously muscular chest again or think of him in deliciously sexy ways.

You will not be alone with him again except in your cabin.

You will wear clothing around him at all times.

You will stop imagining what the rest of him looks like naked.

Chapter Seven

Logan took another slug of his beer then propped his feet up on the edge of the dock railing. This was the life. Peace, quiet, nature, and nothing to do but drink a beer and relax in the setting sun. Today had been a great day, the best he could remember having in years actually.

Usually his days consisted of running around from his apartment to the studio, then stopping to eat somewhere or hauling groceries home. It was a life filled with going all the time but rarely ever taking a moment to enjoy it. But here it was completely different. Of course, he knew everyone was in vacation mode and it wasn't what real life was like, but people being on vacation was a change all on its own. People in the city didn't take vacations often, and if they did, it was to somewhere flashy or noisy. They'd go somewhere there was always something going on, something to do, somewhere to be, needing to be constantly entertained. No one ever went somewhere to simply relax.

This was certainly a relaxing kind of vacation. He loved every second of it. Already today he'd worked out, gone on a firewood run, paddle boarded, played a few rounds of poker and was now waiting to eat a home-cooked dinner and start a bonfire later. Did life get any better than this? The fact that by the end of the year it could be over hit him in the gut with ferocity. He'd just gotten here, hadn't even started his job in the school yet, and already he was dreading the thought of having to leave if things didn't work out teaching or with his gym.

He'd never thought of himself in terms of where he lived making a difference to who he was. After living in a city forever and now seeing what it was like to live in a rural setting, there was no question he was happier here. If his term wasn't extended at the school or if he couldn't figure out a way to open a new training studio in town, he'd have no choice but to go back.

Or was there another choice?

He wasn't qualified to do any other kind of work besides teaching or personal training, but surely he could get a job doing landscaping work or something else that would keep him moving. Something that would keep him in town even if he wasn't doing his dream job. Would any job be fulfilling enough if it meant he could stay here and look at amazing sunsets like this all the time?

Oranges, pinks, and deep purples filled the sky from the surface of the lake to edge of the stars. Never had he seen a sunset like this before. With so much open sky in front of him, he didn't know which section to look at first.

His gaze landed on a figure sitting in a folding lawn chair near the fire pit. Even in the darkening light, he knew it was Tessa, sketchbook on her lap and a charcoal pencil in her hand. She had been there since shortly after returning from the lake. Well, not that one specific spot exactly. She'd moved around. First on the dock where he now sat, then off in the woods on a fallen log that hadn't looked comfortable, and finally siting by the fire that would soon be lit.

What was in that sketchbook of hers? Pictures, obviously, but of what? When she looked around this space that she seemed to simultaneously love and hate, what did she see that was worth immortalizing on paper? He wanted to commit every moment of his time here to memory, but this was all so new and unfamiliar to him. Did she feel the same way, wanting to commit the scenes to paper permanently even though she claimed she couldn't wait to get away from here again? It didn't seem to add up. Curiosity sent him into motion and he wandered over to her, sipping his beer along the way. Did she look at the sunset and think it was as amazing as he did? Or was it another boring end to a day in a small town to her?

He wasn't exactly being sneaky, but he wasn't loud or obvious either. When he neared her chair, almost close enough to see her current page, her head snapped up and her book flipped shut. The look she shot him said he was busted and guilty of spying.

Strangely, seeing how protective she was of her work actually made him feel guilty.

"What are you working on so hard over here?" he asked, taking a seat across from her and setting down his beer.

"Nothing."

"Well, you've been working on nothing for hours."

"Sketches." She folded her hands on top of the book protectively.

"Oh good. That puts to rest the idea that you were doing origami." Grabbing a few logs and some kindling, he started building up the fire pit.

"Why do you care so much what I was sketching?"

"I don't. It's called making polite conversation. That's all."

The kindling caught and he blew on the small flame, making it dance and grow. In a few minutes the larger logs smoldered and he could feel heat radiating out of the pit.

Soon it would be warm and cozy and he was ready for another drink to enjoy fireside.

"I'm going in to grab another beer. You want anything?" he asked as he picked up his empty bottle. "Unless of course it's none of my business what you're drinking tonight and therefore couldn't possibly consider getting it for you."

"I'd love a glass of wine. Thank you."

"Watch the fire while I'm gone, okay?"

"Sure," she said standing and grabbing a long, skinny stick then gently poking at the fire.

When he returned a few minutes later, he handed her the glass of red wine. Waiting for him in his chair was her sketchbook, opened. He sat with it in his lap, taking in all the little details. This was more than a sketch. As he expected, it was a landscape of the cabin and the surrounding woods. She'd done an outstanding job of capturing the atmosphere of the area. The way the light twinkled off the lake and seeped through the branches of the trees, the small animals hiding in the ground cover and leaves, even the hint of fog rising off the surface of the water like it had this morning when he'd gone for his jog. The more he looked, the more details he noticed, including what looked to be the shape of a man, mid-stride, jogging in the woods.

"You did this whole thing when I went for my jog, didn't you?" He didn't wait for her to reply. "It's amazing."

"Thank you," she said, crouching at his side, looking at the sketch with him. "I'm sorry I was bitchy when you asked about my book. I don't like to share my work, especially not until it's finished, but I shouldn't have expected you to know that. I could have told you that instead of being so rude."

She looked so vulnerable and unsure of herself, but she had no reason to be. He wished he had that kind of talent to be protective of. "What made you decide to show me this one?"

She shrugged. "This one seemed finished. I'm sure there are things I could fix, but for a sketch, it's not bad. Good enough to show you anyway. My best stuff is always in paint, not charcoal."

"You don't give yourself enough credit. I wouldn't be able to accomplish something like this if I had ten years to work on it and you probably whipped it up in ten minutes."

"More like thirty, but who's counting?" Her smile played lazily on her lips as she glanced up at him. In the darkness settling around them, her good looks took on a whole new quality. She wasn't only beautiful on the outside, though there was no denying she could be a model, but there was so much more to her. Her eyes twinkled even more as the darkness dilated her pupils and the firelight reflected in them. Her skin looked golden and sun-kissed from their adventure on the lake. And with all the activity of the day, her hair had taken on an unruliness that sent it into a river of curls framing her face and falling to her shoulders in a way that made him long to tangle his fingers in its depths.

She'd opened up herself to him by showing him her sketchbook, a part of herself that was so personal and private that she didn't share it with anyone. Knowing that she'd decided to share it with him touched him in ways he hadn't felt in a long time, if ever. When was the last time a woman had let him in, unguarded and vulnerable, to her deepest most sacred places?

Never.

Tessa had.

Somehow this girl who only yesterday had wanted to throttle him after their accident, and who'd done basically nothing but fight with him since, had suddenly given him a piece of herself. As tempting as it was to flip the page to see more, he carefully closed the book. If she wanted him to see other pictures, she'd show him herself.

Tessa was different.

Tessa challenged him every step of the way. She didn't make anything easy and in fact, most of the time he suspected she was being difficult on purpose. Pushing him away, although why she would do that, he had no idea.

Even though he knew he stood to get nothing but friendship out of this week with her, he couldn't stop himself from wanting to learn more about her. He wanted to dig deeper, find out what made her tick. Part of him knew it was because then he could use it against her to push her buttons so she'd fight with him some more. He liked that fierce, determined, unyielding side of her. And when she fought with him, she got a fire in her eyes that showed him how much passion she had simmering inside. He longed to bring that out of her in any way he could, even if it meant engaging her in another argument. But arguing was the furthest thing from his mind now. Instead, he wished she didn't have a boyfriend so he could pull her onto his lap and kiss her luscious-looking lips and not stop until they turned dark pink and plump and called out his name for more.

But she had a boyfriend.

So rather than act on his emotions, going with his gut, he did the only thing a stand-up kind of guy could do. He handed her sketchbook back and reached for his beer instead. It was an inadequate substitute for what he truly wanted.

"I bet sometime I'll see one of your paintings hanging in a gallery somewhere."

"Thanks," she said, her voice coming out as barely more than a whisper as she looked up at him through her eyelashes.

"Dinner's ready," Martha called as she walked up to the fire pit. In her arms she carried a platter of assorted hotdogs and sausages while Mary, Travis, and Sally held dishes of what looked like potato salad, pasta salad, and coleslaw.

His mouth watered at the sight. "I wish you'd let me

help with this." He wasn't a great cook but he'd like to do something to earn his keep.

"Don't worry. In this family we all take our turn cooking. You'll get your chance before the week is out. But if you have a preference for what meal, feel free to speak up. Otherwise, I'll give you one I'm tired of doing."

"Sounds fair to me. I should probably warn you I'm not a great cook."

"Neither am I, honey." With that she handed him a metal stick and offered him the platter of assorted meats. "Sausage or hot dog. Your choice and done how you like it since you're the one heating it up over the fire. Both are pre-cooked already."

He accepted a sausage and skewered it, making sure it was secure and wouldn't fall into the fire. "Thank you. Everything looks fantastic."

When was the last time he'd cooked on an open campfire? Never. That wasn't something people did in the city. As the flames licked the sausage, his gaze moved to where Tessa was sliding a hotdog onto her stick. Her touch looked gentle as she squeezed the wiener, guiding it down the shaft of the skewer. He swallowed, his throat suddenly feeling dry. Maybe it was all the campfire smoke he'd been sucking in great gulps as he watched. Food was not a turn on to him, or it never had been…until now.

Now the sight of her paying such close attention to the hotdog made him jealous. He could practically imagine how it would feel to have her hands on his body, guiding him gently to where she wanted him.

"What?" she asked. "Why are you looking at me like that?"

"Nothing. Sorry." He coughed to clear his throat and his mind. How long had he'd been staring at her like that? Hopefully not long. "I was watching you handle that wiener."

"Perhaps you should pay attention to your own wiener and stop worrying about the one in my hands." She grinned and arched an eyebrow.

He wasn't completely sure, but her tone sounded slightly different tonight, not the usual wanting to fight with him tone, more of a teasing, almost flirty tone. But there was no way she was flirting with him, not when she had that boyfriend back in the city.

Unless…

Today on the lake, he was sure her story about that guy's job was different, and he was sure that she'd sounded nervous talking about him. In fact, she'd visibly relaxed when the subject had moved on to other things. Why would she act like that unless there was something suspicious about her story, something she didn't want people to figure out?

"Fire. Dude. Earth to Logan." Travis clapped his hands together, laughing when Logan finally pulled his eyes from Tessa.

"Shit!" he blurted.

His nicely secured sausage was currently on fire. He pulled the stick out of the pit and blew on the flames to put them out without splattering hot grease on himself or anyone else. When they were finally out, all that remained on his stick was a shriveled and blackened pathetic looking piece of meat.

"You may as well grab a new one," Martha said.

"I think we should make him eat that one. Penance for not paying attention. Didn't you always say we had to be extra careful around the fire, Dad?" Tessa asked, her voice sounding far more innocent than her expression said it should be.

She was a devious one. No wonder they referred to her as the rebel of the family. While everyone else was more than happy to welcome him into the fold, she took every opportunity to ride him, push his buttons, and spar with him. And so far he'd taken every opportunity she'd presented to encourage her behavior.

After today, he'd definitely encourage her to ride him tonight. Hard.

His balls tingled with the idea.

If only he could figure out what was up with that boyfriend situation for real because he couldn't shake the notion there was more to the story.

"You're right, Tessa-bear. I should eat this wiener since I'm the one that burned it. However, I like your mom's idea better." He retrieved a new sausage from the table. This time he kept it close enough to warm up but far enough from the flames that there was no chance for it to burn.

He watched her expression while they chatted. It seemed her face gave away more truth than her words.

"So when you and Richard meet for dinner after work, do you usually meet him uptown for dinner? There's this great little place I used to go on the Upper East Side called Frieda's. It'd be close to his office building."

Her gaze darted from the fire to his and around to the rest of their group. "Um, yeah. We eat up there a lot actually since it's easier for me to come to him than for him to pick me up. I don't think we've ever had Frieda's though." She giggled as if she was nervous.

"You should ask him. They have great lunch specials for cheap and service is fast. I bet he's eaten there with his colleagues before. I'm curious if he likes it as much as I do." Hearing the words he knew he wasn't talking about liking a restaurant. It was Tessa he liked.

"I'll do that," she said quickly with a smile.

"I thought Richard worked on Wall Street," Mary said, chiming into the conversation exactly how Logan hoped someone would.

"Me too. Wasn't that why he couldn't take the week off? That big important finance job?" Sally asked.

"Oh, did I say Wall Street?" She giggled again and this time it definitely sounded nervous. "I guess I wasn't clear. I should've said he works on the Upper East Side but often has to travel down to Wall Street for meetings and whatnot." She thought fast on her feet. Apparently she was no stranger to getting herself out of a tough spot with a little creative fiction.

When her gaze locked with his this time, he could tell she was hiding the truth—there was no boyfriend in the city. Maybe the rest of her family hadn't figured it out yet, but he'd caught her in the lie.

He smirked when she shook her head so subtly he almost missed it. He nodded once, a silent communication—saying he knew her secret and he'd keep his mouth shut. For now.

Later he'd find out why she lied, but for now he'd let her secret linger. Honestly, he didn't give a damn why she'd made up a boyfriend. All he cared about was what this meant for him and the rest of his vacation, in a cabin, alone with her.

Tessa was single.

Chapter Eight

Tessa didn't know how Logan figured out she'd lied about Rich—or Richard or Dick, or whatever the hell she'd said his name was—but however he'd managed it, it didn't matter anymore. He knew she'd lied. Now the question was, why had he kept her secret? And if he did agree to keep his mouth shut, would he expect something from her in return? What would make him stay on her side when he could so easily confide the truth in his friend Travis?

Tessa had no idea. Thankfully, her family didn't seem any more aware of her fictional romantic life than they had earlier, and Logan seemed content to drop the subject. He'd been the one who'd brought up her fake boyfriend to begin with and now that he caught her in her lie, he'd moved on to other topics.

"I'm looking forward to working with the kids, but it'll be different for me," he said. "I'm used to working with adults who can make the choice for themselves about whether or not they want to live a healthy lifestyle. Now I'll be encouraging kids to make good choices on their own while being able to show them how much stronger, faster, and more flexible they can be if they apply themselves in my class."

"Sounds like you'll be a positive influence in the school," Mary said, smiling. It wasn't her flirting smile, but the fact that she was paying so much attention to Logan suddenly annoyed Tessa.

Hands off, sis. She shook her head. *Whoa. Where did that come from?* Shocked at her own thoughts, she focused on the fire again and tried to ignore their conversation.

"Thanks. I hope to start a program for the faculty while I'm there too. I know it's only for six months, but I feel like I could leave a lasting impression if I can get them motivated to make some positive changes too."

"What did you have in mind?" her mom asked.

"I thought I'd start with a walking program during lunch or even before school if there was interest. And since I know the students usually only get physical education once or twice a week, I thought it might be fun to start a daily break where everyone in the school pauses to do a short, easy guided exercise routine. Simple stuff, like stretching and jumping jacks and maybe even an easy yoga move or two. Everyone can do mountain pose, can't they?"

"Tessa probably can't," Sally piped up from somewhere in the darkness.

"I *can* do the mountain pose." Tessa jutted her chin out.

"Do it. I dare you," Mary said.

"Fine. I will." She stood with her shoulders back and her eyes focused on Logan and acted as if staring at him intensely didn't make her knees weak. "What's the mountain pose?"

They all laughed, except for Logan who stood on one leg with the other knee bent and at an angle while his foot rested against the knee of his straightened leg. As if that wasn't enough, He raised his arms above his head and brought them down in front of his chest in a sort of prayer pose. And he did it all without a single wobble, flinch, or sway.

Sure. I can do that too. No problem.

As she attempted the same pose, she locked her eyes on his, refusing to be intimidated by his stability. She successfully balanced on one foot with only a mild wobble, sliding her opposite foot up her leg until her knee was bent and at an angle similar to his. Maybe it was a little lower, but whatever, close enough.

"I did it." She continued to balance with her arms outstretched to the sides, while her toes gripped the insides of her shoes as if they alone could make her stay upright.

Logan came to stand in front of her. "Now you need to raise your arms above your head, like this." He resumed the yoga position with ease and she tried to mirror his arm movements.

As soon as her arms were above her head, it was as if her ankle forgot how to do its job. The wiggle of instability started up her leg and before she could put her hands into the proper prayer pose, she fell toward the fire, her leg shooting out to the side in a feeble attempt at counter-balance. But it wasn't her extended leg that saved her from the flames.

It was Logan's strong arms wrapping around her torso and pulling her back to safety.

Her skin felt fifty degrees hotter as she found her footing, all the while with his hands on her back, squeezing her gently against his broad chest. His biceps were large and firm in her hands as she clung to him, not even having realized she'd grabbed him. Now that she'd noticed, she couldn't focus on anything but his taut skin beneath her fingers.

"I'm fine. You can let go of me." She made her voice as confident as she could, hoping none of her family would hear her nervousness and perceive it to be because of being in Logan's arms. Because it wasn't. Feeling his strong arms around her like she was getting a hug from a buff teddy bear who smelled like a mix of campfire and sex had absolutely no effect on her whatsoever. None.

"You're welcome." He smirked. "I think you should do yoga with me some time. You could use the practice, and learning some basic balance would be beneficial too."

"What makes you a yoga expert?"

"I teach yoga." His eyebrows scrunched together a little making a crease between them. "Actually, I used to teach yoga at my gym before I had to close the doors."

The sadness in his voice created a pit in her stomach. She hadn't expected that kind of response to his emotion, but it was as if her body knew he was hurting and instinctually wanted to comfort him. She wanted to pull him close, wrap herself around him, and let him pour his heart out to her. Instead, she took a step back and out of his arms. She wouldn't get caught up in his world, not if his world was in Cutter's Creek.

"Sorry to hear about your gym, but I don't want or need yoga classes. Thanks, but I'm fine the way I am."

He leveled her with his gaze. "I'll remember that the next time you're headed for the fire."

She stared right back, unblinking. "Please do."

Her mother brought out ingredients to make s'mores and Tessa eagerly grabbed a marshmallow, skewered it, and stuck it in the fire. As she sat back in her chair, she shivered. It had been warmer standing so close to the fire.

And in his arms.

Shut it.

"Well, I think your idea sounds fantastic. I hope the school goes for it," Mary said.

"Thank you. I hope so too." The smile he sent toward Mary sent a fire bolt of jealousy shooting through Tessa's chest.

No. Not jealousy.

Mary needed a strong talking to if she planned to keep

flirting so blatantly with Logan. He wasn't right for her. He was a muscle head while Mary was a sensitive, caring girl who needed someone else equally as kind. Not someone who loved to push buttons and irritate the people around him, like Logan. No. Logan needed someone strong and feisty who could stand up for herself, someone who wasn't afraid to speak her mind. Someone like Tessa.

No. Not like me.

Tessa pulled her marshmallow from the fire when it turned a golden brown, trapped it between the two graham crackers and chocolate she'd pre-assembled and squished it gently until the gooey white fluff threatened to spill out the sides. The sticky fluff was sweet on her tongue as she licked the edges.

Taking a bite, she sighed and let her eyelids flutter closed as she chewed. Crisp crackers mixed with melted milk chocolate and creamy marshmallow rolled around on her tongue, tantalizing her taste buds. Each bite made the flavor in her mouth stronger, richer, more satisfying. Was there anything better?

She missed being able to do this any night of the week now that she lived in a tiny apartment. Growing up, they'd often light a small fire in a fire pit in the back yard throughout the week and would sit out there to watch the sunset over the mountains, have drinks, and make s'mores. But that wasn't something she could do in the city.

Licking her lips clean, she debated having another.

Her gaze fell to Logan. He held a s'more in his hand, but it was as if he'd forgotten it was there. Instead, he stared at her so intensely she could almost feel his gaze raking over her entire body. She pulled her lower lip between her teeth, gently scraping off a tiny bit of chocolate. As she did, Logan's mouth fell open slightly.

Something about the way he looked at her made her pulse

pound in her limbs, making them tingle with excitement. *Get a grip.* She would not let her body's chemical response overrule what she knew in her brain she wanted. Clearly, she was tired from the long day and needed to put her overreacting body to bed before it made decisions she didn't agree with.

Like licking her lips again to see if Logan noticed.

If his eyes widening and his tongue touching his lips was any indication, he did.

But that shouldn't matter. She had a fake boyfriend, and Logan was a dangerous temptation that threatened to drag her back to town if she let her libido make decisions for her.

Stop it. Bed. Now.

"I'm beat," she said standing. "I'm off to bed for the night. See you all in the morning."

Gathering her sketchbook and pencils, she quickly made her way back to the cabin. Once safely inside, she flopped down on her bed and buried her head in her pillow. She wasn't one to run and hide in her room, but with Logan around eyeing her constantly, she didn't see any other place to be. Every time he looked at her like that, she felt something inside come to life, which was exactly the last thing she wanted to happen with a guy from town.

Eventually she did want to meet someone, fall in love, and live happily ever after. First, she wanted to focus on her art and establishing herself in her career. Then she would worry about finding someone and settling down. By then she'd be in the social circles in the city and that's the kind of guy she wanted to meet. Not someone who'd left the city to move to Nowheresville.

Why couldn't her body listen to reason and stop getting all tingly and gooey every time Logan so much as looked at her? God help her if he decided to touch her again. She'd barely been able to think straight the couple of times it had happened so far, but her reaction seemed to be getting progressively worse. At least she had her fake boyfriend to fall back on, since there was no way a stand up guy like Logan would cross that line. Her boyfriend might be fake, but he provided a real buffer between herself and Logan and all the temptation that went along with him.

"A few more days then Logan will be out of my space for good."

"Sorry. I didn't realize I'd been in your space. Thought I did a pretty good job of staying on my side of the room actually."

She groaned into her pillow, wishing it could swallow her whole so she wouldn't have to turn and face the man in question. Why couldn't he stay at the fire tonight like the rest of her family? Why did he have to keep following her back to the cabin? She wanted to have a little time for herself where she didn't have to pretend to be anything: in a relationship, successfully pursuing her art, blissfully happy and fulfilled.

Reluctantly, she sat up. "I didn't realize you'd followed me." She didn't apologize for her words since there was nothing wrong with what she'd said. Not to mention that the bigger bitch she was, the less likely he was to stick around.

"I didn't follow you. This is my cabin too, remember?" He sat on his bed and slipped his shoes off then leaned back against the wall looking casual, but not at all like he had a purpose for coming back to the cabin so early.

"Yes, and I can see why you were in a hurry to come back here and relax. There's no way you could unwind around a soothing campfire." Why was he here exactly?

"True, but I could say the same about you."

"I came back because I'm tired and I planned on going to bed," she said.

"I thought maybe you'd come back here to chat with your boyfriend since I haven't seen you call him once since arriving."

She swallowed. There was that look in his eyes again, the one saying he might not believe her boyfriend story as easily as the others did.

"I planned to call him, but I guess privacy was too much to hope for, wasn't it?" Maybe he'd leave her alone to make her supposed call and she'd conveniently be in bed with the lights off and "sleeping" by the time he got back.

"Don't let me stop you. I'll go wash up." He said the words, yet made no motion to actually move.

Sighing, she picked up her phone. "I'll text him instead. I wouldn't want to disturb your beauty rest."

She quickly typed out a message to Mary asking if she wanted to join her for a hike to lookout point tomorrow. It would be fun to spend time hanging out with Mary, and as an added bonus, it would get her away from Logan for a few hours. She hit send.

Clicking on her email while she got a good signal, she held her breath when she saw the name of a gallery pop up. Her pulse raced as she opened the message, then slowed when she saw the one paragraph rejection. It was the same as the others—too similar to other artists, not unique, missing that something special. She still had one more gallery to hear from, and surely they would give her a chance.

Sighing, she tossed her phone upside down on the bed as if she wasn't hiding something, then got up to go brush her teeth. "Sometimes it takes Richard a few minutes to return my texts if he's busy working. I'll wash up now so you can go in there." She looked at him pointedly as she moved across the room.

With the water running in the sink, she brushed her teeth and tried not to read too much into Logan coming back to the cabin early. Surely he hadn't come back to annoy her. It was entirely possible he was finding it awkward to spend so much time with her family when he barely knew them. Or he might be genuinely tired since he was used to the city life and not so much fresh mountain air. By the time she'd finished with her teeth, she was completely convinced she was overreacting to him being in the cabin. It was simply a product of their rocky relationship.

Not that they had a relationship.

She pulled open the bathroom door only to find Logan leaning against the doorframe, a smirk gracing his face. If she hadn't been paying attention, she would have walked right into him. As it was, she barely stopped before making contact with his chest.

Damn it. Every time she was up close to him, his proximity played with her senses, clouded her brain, and made her want to forget her reasoning for staying away.

"Can I help you?" she asked, crossing her arms as an added barrier between them.

"You got a text and I thought you'd be anxious to hear back from your man so I walked your phone over to the bathroom. Of course, along the way I couldn't help but notice that the text was from your sister. That is unless Richard the Dick also goes by Mary."

He handed her the phone and she held it close to her chest while trying to maintain her composure. It was one thing to put up with his questions and him being in her space, but it was completely unacceptable for him to go through her private belongings.

"You had no right to read my text. From my boyfriend or from my sister."

"You're absolutely right."

"Good, so we're in agreement that you're officially an asshole." She moved to walk around him, but he sidestepped, blocking her path. On instinct she put up her hands up to brace herself against running into him. His pecs were as firm and sculpted as she remembered. Without permission, her hands roamed down his sleek torso, gliding over ridges and plains.

"I wouldn't say that."

"What would you say?" She withdrew her hands and attempted to step the other way around him and was blocked once more.

"That I was curious who you were actually texting since I knew it couldn't possibly be your boyfriend."

"That's a pretty big assumption considering I'd told you I was texting him. Not exactly roommate-like for someone who moments ago claimed to not be in my space. Why didn't you take my word for it?"

"Because you don't have a boyfriend."

The accusation hung in the air. She didn't respond, silently refusing to confirm or deny his comment. He remained steadfastly mute as well, not giving an inch on his claim to her relationship status. Why couldn't he let it go? "What's it to you?"

He shrugged but didn't say anything, simply held her gaze, raising an eyebrow, questioningly.

"I don't have to tell you anything."

"True, but you should admit it." His smirk grew. "Wouldn't it be easier if you didn't have to be deceitful even in your own cabin for the rest of the week?"

True. It would be nice if she could have this one spot to relax. And with Logan seeming to be everywhere she was when she left the cabin, it would be nice if she could be herself with him at least. Hiding it from everyone was hard. But if she gave in and admitted the truth, what would that mean for the thing that definitely *wasn't* going on between her and Logan? That feeling she definitely *didn't* feel spring up inside her when he was around? That tingling and heat *not* pooling low in her belly whenever she smelled his spicy cologne mixing with campfire smoke and lake water. Would she still be able to push all of that nonsense aside if there wasn't the fake boyfriend buffer anymore?

She met his gaze and could clearly see that he knew the truth even without her admission. He wanted to make her say the words. "Fine."

"Fine, what?" he asked, his eyebrow arching again.

"I might have exaggerated the boyfriend story."

"Why'd you lie?"

"Because if I told the truth, they'd never shut up about how I should move home and marry a guy from town. I hoped for a week of peace, but I guess that's never happening with my family, is it?"

"What's wrong with a guy from town?" His voice rose with defensiveness. "Your family is nice. I can only imagine at least some of the men in this town are okay too."

Some might be nice, but not all. And that wasn't a conversation she was having with Logan now, or ever if she could help it. The past was the past and that's how she wanted to keep things. "I've had my fill of small town life."

"Vague."

It was her turn to shrug. "You're so full of questions. How about you answer one for me?" she asked.

"Fire away," he said, his mouth set in a firm line.

"Why do you care so much that I lied about having a boyfriend?"

"Because if there's a guy back in the city I have no choice but to respect that."

She swallowed, suddenly feeling nervousness and excitement mix in her stomach. "And if there's no guy?" Her voice came out as a whisper.

Logan lifted her chin with his fingers then slid his hand along her jaw and into the hair at the base of her neck. "If there's no boyfriend, then you're single. And I'm single. And we're all alone in this cozy cabin every night."

"So? I'm still not interested. Sorry to burst your big ego bubble." The lump of anticipation in her throat made it feel as if her airway was closing, but she sucked in a staggered breath.

She tried to step away but before she could, he had her pressed against the doorframe. A tiny gasp escaped her parted lips at the pleasure of him leaning into her body in all the right places. How many times had she imagined a scenario like this happening? Many. But Logan wasn't a fantasy. He was real and felt better than anything her imagination could ever come up with. Why she'd been fighting the attraction she'd felt for him since meeting him on the twisting mountain road escaped her realm of thinking right now.

"You might claim you're not interested, but I'm pretty sure that's another lie. And if you're single and willing, and I'm single and wanting, then there's nothing to stop me from doing this."

He brushed his lips against hers, lingering only long enough to cause her to arch into him involuntarily. Feeling as if she was suffocating, she tried to suck in a breath. When she did, his tongue swept across her bottom lip and she trembled.

He pulled back, his eyes heavy-lidded. "I'm pretty sure I know the truth about what you want too. So tell me once and for all, is there a guy in the city waiting for you?" His gaze penetrated hers, intense and full of need, longing.

"You can't say anything to my family. They'll never leave me alone to make my own decisions."

"I'll keep your secret."

She relaxed in his arms. His thumb brushed across her lower lip, and she fought to control the tremble of nerves his touch brought to life.

"If…" He paused.

Biting her lip, she prayed he wouldn't ask for something in return she couldn't give. "If what?" she whispered.

"If you'll promise to be one hundred percent real and

honest with me when we're alone. I get that you don't want your family to know. They're well meaning, but even I can see how much of a hard time they give you over everything. If they knew the truth, I think you're right about how they would react and I'd hate to see you go crazy over it. So around them you can keep up the charade."

She nodded, not trusting her voice to stay strong and steady.

"But when we're alone, you're single, and you won't write me off because I decided to move to Cutter's Creek instead of staying in the city. You'll respect my decision as much as you want your family to respect yours."

Well, when he said it like that… She hadn't realized she'd acted hypocritically. It wasn't fair to him anymore than it was fair to her that her family tried to pressure her into moving home. She thought she was a better person, but apparently the meddling apple didn't fall far from the busy-bodied tree.

"Deal?" He inched forward slightly and her breath caught in her throat at his nearness. He was even hotter up close. There was something so sexy about his confident ability to take charge of the situation.

She licked her lips while finding her voice, never taking her gaze from his. "Deal." The word was barely out of her mouth before his lips were on hers again. Heat rocketed through her body making her toes tingle with desire. His kiss was deeper, needier than the first, and she wanted more.

A few seconds later, Logan broke the kiss, his chest rising and falling with quick breaths that matched hers. He looked at her for another few moments then stepped away and went to lay on his bed as if nothing had happened.

Her head spun as if she'd drunk an entire bottle of wine. Walking back to her bed, she felt in a fog. Not wanting to show him or admit to herself how much she'd been affected by his kiss, she picked up her book from the nightstand as casually as she could and mindlessly stared at the pages, flipping once in a while to look as if she were actually reading.

Somehow, in an odd twist of fate she hadn't seen coming, she no longer had a fake boyfriend but instead now had a very real crush on the sexy man lying a few feet away. A man who recently moved to the town she couldn't wait to leave.

This couldn't be good.

But that kiss had been anything but bad.

Chapter Nine

Logan poured a coffee to take with him back to his cabin. Being in nature was amazing, but he could do with a few comforts from home. His smoothies were something he rarely went more than a few days without. Coffee was great quick energy, but after a good workout like the one he'd had this morning, he could use the sustained energy his protein-enriched smoothies would've offered.

"Anything on the schedule for today?" he asked Martha.

She paused her organizing of the pantry momentarily to answer him. "Joe and I might head out on the lake for a bit. James mentioned running into town to check on Tessa's car."

"Tessa and I have plans to hike up to the lookout," Mary said from the adjoining room. "You're welcome to join us. Of course, you already got a workout by the looks of it, so maybe you don't want to hike up a mountain too."

"Sounds like fun. When are we leaving?"

"Half an hour. Tessa was packing a backpack and then meeting me here."

"Great. I'll rinse off quickly and grab my stuff."

He left with his coffee, walking as fast as he could without spilling it. A hike up the mountain with Tessa sounded great. Although it would be better if they were alone, he'd take what he could get.

Last night had been a good moment between them. Finally, he knew that she was single and when they were in private she wouldn't pretend that she wasn't. She'd be real with him, and he couldn't wait. Their kiss was the tip of something more, something amazing.

He wished she didn't have to pretend to be in a relationship around her family either. All that made him want to do was hang out in their cabin constantly. But he also wanted to explore the area, hang out with Travis and the rest of the family, and enjoy everything that camping had to offer.

Like Tessa in a bikini on the paddleboard.

If only they'd had their conversation about her fake boyfriend before that moment. He definitely wouldn't have let her off his board so quickly. He would've kept her there, between his legs and in his arms, asked her more questions about her life, and gotten to know everything about her.

As the door to the cabin swung open, he glanced around the room, but Tessa was nowhere to be seen. Setting his cup down on his bedside table, he stripped off his clothes and walked naked to the shower. As the water warmed, he shaved his morning scruff. He might be in the mountains, but he had no desire to look like a mountain man. Stubble he could handle, a beard, no way. They itched.

Logan showered and dressed in record time, not wanting to hold up the expedition to the lookout, wherever that was. Pulling his backpack out from under the bed, he made sure he had a few essentials like protein bars, a small first aid kit, and a Swiss Army knife. He didn't know how far they were hiking today, but it was a good idea to go prepared for anything.

He finished his coffee on the way and rinsed his cup in the

sink before grabbing a few bottles of water for his backpack. Outside, Tessa and Mary were pulling their packs onto their shoulders when he walked up.

"Hey," he said. "I didn't keep you waiting, did I?"

"Nope. We were getting ready to head out," Mary said, smiling.

Tessa glanced between the two of them. "Are you coming with us?"

"Yep."

"Why?"

"Rude," Mary said. "I invited him to join us."

"Well, why did you do that?" Tessa asked, her hands on her hips.

"Because he's never been before. I didn't think it was a girl's only kind of trip or anything."

"You sure know how to make a guy feel welcome," Logan said, trying not to show his amusement. He didn't know Tessa's exact motivation for wanting her space, but he had a few good guesses. One, was that kiss. Maybe she liked it more than she wanted to. Two, having him around was probably a big reminder of how much she liked that kiss. Possibly she even wanted to kiss him again but was fighting it. If her gaze dropping to his lips repeatedly was any indication, she was thinking about them a lot more than he thought. Already he'd caught her a few times and he'd only been with them for a minute. And lastly, if he was around, there was always a chance he could spill her fake boyfriend secret, not that he would.

Her secret was safe with him. He wouldn't tell. He'd already pissed her off once with the whole car accident and had only recently won her favor. He wasn't about to risk getting on her bad side again. Her good side was so much better.

"I promise I won't get in the way, and I'll turn a deaf ear

to any girl talk. Mary invited me, and the thought of seeing the view sounded too good to pass up, but I won't go if you want time alone with your sister. If I had siblings, I'd probably want to spend time alone with them bonding too."

He could practically see his words sinking in as Tessa's stiff posture eased. She bit her lower lip, looking up at him sheepishly. "Of course you can come."

They started up the path at a leisurely pace, clearly in no rush to reach the top or wherever the lookout was. After a few minutes, they were so far into the brush already that he couldn't see the cabins or hear people in the campground. The only noise was their footfalls, the rustling leaves, and birds. The wide trail allowed them to walk side-by-side. Its gradual incline was enough to make his breathing increase marginally, but not so much that it was any kind of struggle. He'd walked a harder incline on his treadmill. The girls, however, seemed to be having a more challenging time. Already, they breathed loud and fast.

"You girls okay?" he asked.

"Fine," Tessa answered.

"Actually, can we stop for a minute?" Mary asked. "I want to find a walking stick. Once the path gets steeper, I'll need it."

"Sounds like a good idea for all of us," he said. And it would give them a chance to rest before they started up again.

Tessa wandered off the trail a few steps to retrieve a stick that came up to her shoulders. Logan looked around for a few minutes before finding one. He had no question about being able to hike the steepest sections even without the help, but he wanted to be part of the group. So if the girls were using walking sticks, he would too.

He was about to suggest they continue when Mary's cell phone rang.

"Hey, James. What's up?" she asked, perching on the edge of a large boulder. "Oh crap. I forgot about that. I'm about twenty minutes up the lookout trail with Tessa and Logan. I can probably be back in half that. Can you wait for me?"

Apparently, Mary was supposed to be in two places at once. The thought of her heading back to camp by herself on the trail didn't sit well with him.

"Sorry, guys. I've got to cut my hiking trip short," Mary said after ending her call. "I forgot James and I are supposed to cook tonight. I have to head back and run into town to pick up the stuff we need."

"Can't James go by himself? He is an adult now and can buy a few groceries." Tessa's voice sounded simultaneously annoyed and nervous. An odd combination.

"He could, but then we'd likely end up eating Doritos and beef jerky for dinner."

Tessa groaned. "True. Remember last time he was in charge of the meal himself? Nothing says camping like fish sticks with macaroni and cheese for dinner. It was as if he forgot we weren't a bunch of five year olds."

"See why I need to go?" Mary laughed. "I'll make sure we eat something decent tonight."

"Can we walk you back?" Logan asked, hoping she'd say yes. Hiking alone could be dangerous.

"No. I'll be fine. I've hiked this trail a thousand times and I've got everything I need in my pack." Mary pounded the end of her walking stick into the ground as if testing its strength. "Besides, it'll take me half the time to get back and you'd have to turn around and start your hike all over."

"Are you sure? It's no trouble?" Tessa added, shooting a sideways glance toward Logan. "Maybe we should head back too."

"It's your favorite place here. Take Logan. It's an amazing view and one you shouldn't miss because I have to go grocery shopping." Without waiting for more discussion on the subject, Mary gave them a huge smile and started back down the trail, calling over her shoulder. "Have fun. Don't hurry back. Dinner will be late tonight!"

As Mary disappeared around a bend, he turned to face Tessa. He grabbed his own walking stick and nodded toward the trail leading the opposite way of Mary. "Ready?"

Tessa stared after Mary for another few seconds. "This way," she said with a shrug.

He walked alongside her, easily keeping her pace. A few minutes of silence felt like a million. Tessa sighed every minute or so, and each one sounded progressively more annoyed. Finally, he couldn't take it anymore. "You seem really irritated to be hiking with me. We can turn back if you want."

She didn't respond.

"Will you tell me what's bothering you?"

"Nothing's bothering me."

He laughed. "Famous words said by every annoyed female in history."

"I'm sorry. It's not you, but I can't believe Mary bailed on us."

"I don't think she meant to. Besides, it's still fun to hike this trail, isn't it? I promise I'll be good company. And if it will make you feel more comfortable, I'll even call you Tessa-bear so you feel like your family is here with you and you're not alone in the woods with a guy who's basically a stranger."

"First, don't you dare call me that name. It's one that's been around since I was a kid and I've hated it my whole life. And secondly, you're not exactly a stranger anymore."

He smiled as her tone and mood shifted to something more upbeat and friendly. "Don't forget how I saved you while paddle boarding," he added, goading her on.

She scoffed. "You did not save me. In fact, you're the reason I ended up in the water to begin with."

He ignored her. "And let's not forget the kiss. That's not something strangers do." No way could he forget that moment. The feeling of her lips on his was burned into his memory like they'd been branded on his brain.

Tessa stumbled when her foot slipped on the path. He reached out and grabbed her upper arm, steadying her. "I'm fine," she insisted, shaking her arm loose and starting up the trail again.

"So why exactly do you hate your nickname so much?"

"Because it's childish."

"Lots of people have nicknames they're given as children and they sort of cling to them, cherish them. Why don't you? There must be more to it."

"It's a childish nickname that makes me feel like I'm still a kid. And every time I tell them not to call me that anymore, they ignore me and do it anyway. It's another way they don't see me as an adult. They don't listen to me or respect my opinion."

Now that made sense, but she was probably being a little hard on her family. They'd seemed nothing but loving and kind the whole time he'd been around.

"What about you? Any nicknames you had growing up?"

He shook his head. "My parents weren't nickname kind of people. They took life seriously. Always worrying about everything."

"Guess you're lucky on that account then. I'd take no nickname over the one I've been cursed with."

"I think you're the one to be envied. You have a family who loves you."

"And meddles in my life and constantly nags me to move home."

"Because they want you close by. You're lucky to have a family who cares."

"You want them? You can borrow them for a few years." She had no idea what he'd give for a family like hers. "Did your parents care when you moved out of the city to the middle of nowhere?"

His heart ached in his chest. Even after all these years, it still hurt. "Nope. They've got nothing to say about it. They're not around anymore."

"Not around as in they moved or…"

"Back when I was about seventeen my mom got breast cancer." His breath burned in his chest as the elevation climbed and the trail got steeper. A sweat broke out on his back.

Tessa's hand slipped into his and squeezed. He held her tight, his large hand engulfing her tiny one. The contact felt good, comforting. As if having her touch made his story easier to tell.

"She started treatment right away and the cancer was small so she beat it and went into remission. I remember they were so happy, it was like a weight had lifted off them and they suddenly had a new outlook on life. They smiled more and stopped being so serious all the time. It was awesome."

"It's amazing what a little perspective can do, right?"

"Yup. So they decided to go on a huge trip around the world. I was about to graduate high school so I stayed home. They were somewhere in the Amazon when they went missing. They went into the jungle, but never came back out."

"I had no idea. I'm so sorry for your loss, Logan."

The tough shell that seemed to constantly surround her finally cracked. For the first time he got a glimpse of the woman she kept so closely guarded.

The pain of losing his parents had lessened over the years but there were moments when he still hurt. Telling Tessa about them made his emotions surprisingly raw. And yet she made him feel completely comfortable in sharing his story. Most of the time, he glossed over what happened saying they died, period. But with Tessa it was different. He wanted her to know the whole story. He felt compelled to be completely honest with her the same way he wanted her to be completely honest with him.

"How did you go on to become so successful after suffering a loss like that? I think I would have curled into a ball and stayed there."

"Well, I don't know how successful I've become given that I had to shut down my business and become a temporary gym teacher instead." He chuckled, but nothing about his situation was all that funny. "I guess I kept going because I knew that's what my parents would want."

They started up the steepest part of the trail so far. "With everything you've been through, you have an amazingly positive outlook on life. I haven't heard one negative thing out of your mouth all week. I don't know how you do it, but I should probably start taking notes." She tried to laugh but was breathing too hard.

Even he had to admit this part of the trail was tough. "Life's too short to wallow in what isn't. So I focus on what is and what could be instead. Enjoy the moment, but plan for the future too."

Conversation fell away as the trail difficulty intensified even more. Tessa never stopped or complained as they climbed. The path was so narrow they had to go single file. If he hadn't had to concentrate so hard on his steps, he would have taken more time to enjoy the view ahead of him. As it was, he could barely enjoy Tessa's rear swaying in front of his eyes.

The terrain suddenly flattened out onto a plateau. Without the incline, he realized how hard his legs had been working. His quads quivered with the sustained exertion. He could only imagine how Tessa's quads must feel right now… He could almost feel the heat of her thighs on his fingertips. They were probably soft and smooth and muscular.

"The lookout spot is over there, behind that outcropping

of rocks."

A pasture of green opened up before them. It wasn't huge, maybe only a couple hundred feet in every direction, but it was large enough to be spared the shade of the tree canopy. Running through the middle was a small river with a five-foot waterfall that emptied into a pond before the water continued over the edge of the mountain they'd climbed.

"This is gorgeous. I can't believe there's anything better up here than this place." Seriously, if they'd climbed the whole way to see the lookout point, and she'd never even mentioned this beautiful spot, he couldn't guess how stunning the view from the lookout must be. Sweat trickled down his back. The thought of going for a dip to cool off was too good to pass up. "I'm sweating like crazy. I'm going to take a swim to rinse off. Want to join me?" he asked, pulling his shirt over his head and walking toward the pond.

"I didn't bring a swim suit," she said, following him.

"Me either, but I'm not about to let that stop me." He stopped at the water's edge and toed off his shoes, then peeled off his socks. He paused with his hands on his waistband. "If you don't want to see the rest, you better look away."

He didn't miss the pink of her cheeks as she turned her back. Her coloring had nothing to do with the heat or their hike, he was sure of it. It was the same pink hue that had tinged her cheeks a couple of other times when he'd been bare-chested in front of her. Seeing him without a shirt caused a strong reaction in her, even if she didn't want to admit it.

"You're leaving underwear on, right?" she asked.

"Wrong. Hiking back with soaking wet boxers would lead to way too much chaffing of important parts. I'd rather go nude here."

"Oh," she whispered.

He stripped down, leaving his clothes in a pile on the dry riverbed. The water was cold as he waded in then submerged fully, and for a moment he worried about shrinkage. But Tessa probably wouldn't get close enough to him to notice anyway. It was more refreshing than he'd imagined. Instantly, his body temp dropped and his energy revived itself. "You can turn around," he said.

"How is it in there?" Tessa asked. She pulled her shirt away from her stomach, making the material flutter, fanning her overheated skin.

"Better than it looks. Stop being a prude and get in. I'm sure your bra and panties are no skimpier than that bikini you wore the other day."

"I'm not a prude. And if I come in with my panties on, won't I end up hiking in discomfort too?"

"Good point. You should come in naked. I'll be honest. The cold water swirling around my junk feels pretty fantastic. You're missing out."

She took off her sneakers and socks and dipped a toe into the water. "Swear you'll be a gentleman and not look until I tell you it's okay. And you'll keep your distance. Deal?"

"Deal," he said with a wink before turning his back.

Chapter Ten

Tessa hesitated with her thumbs looped into the elastic of her panties. So far Logan had kept his word and hadn't turned around. But would he continue to be good? The thought of his gaze raking across her naked body made her hotter than the sun beating down on her bare skin.

"Are you in yet?" he asked.

"No, don't turn around," she said.

Pushing aside her last ounce of hesitation, she stepped out of her panties and tucked them into the pocket of her pants, then added her bra to the mix. She couldn't stop the instinct to cover herself with one arm across her breasts. She attempted to cover the rest of herself but quickly gave up. She needed more hands.

But not Logan's hands.

Giving in to the moment, she let her arms hang by her sides and stood completely uncovered. It was only skin, right? Besides, the water would cover her as soon as she got herself into it.

Embrace nature.

Her body might be hot and in need of cooling off, but that didn't mean the water didn't feel damned cold. "I thought you said this was refreshing."

"It is. If you'd stop being a baby and get in, your body would adjust to the temperature faster."

"I am getting in."

Cool spring water rose up her thighs. When it crested her hips, she shrieked.

"Are you okay?" Logan asked, simultaneously turning and reaching for her.

She shrieked louder and dropped into the water, her knees hitting the bottom like a cement block. "I told you not to turn around!" The cold water now hovered around her shoulders, almost stealing her breath while she adjusted to the temperature.

"But you yelped and I thought you needed help or hurt yourself," he said, shrugging. "I was prepared to save you."

"Gee, thanks."

He grunted. "How was I to know you'd make that sound because of a little cold water? You could've fallen or twisted your ankle."

"Well, I didn't. And I couldn't help the noise. The water is cold and my body was hot and…"

His gaze dipped down as if he could see through the water to her naked flesh. "Yes, it was," he said in a tone so low it was almost a whisper.

What did that mean? He didn't see anything, did he?

Her head spun with the thought that he'd seen her naked breasts. *But hey, why not? He's already seen my ass so why not give him a peek of my boobs too?*

"You didn't see anything, right?" she asked, resisting the urge to cover herself. The water did that job for her, didn't it? She couldn't see anything below his waist where the water line hit him—not that she was looking—so he must not be able to see her either. At least, that's what she'd keep telling herself, since climbing out of the water wasn't an option. He'd definitely get an eyeful then.

"Not really." He looked her in the eyes and she instantly knew the truth.

He saw my boobs.

As if in response to the confirmation, her nipples beaded. Damn it, they wanted his attention. Well, they weren't going to get it. Tessa swam deeper into the water. Getting involved with Logan was not an option if she planned to keep her ties to Cutter's Creek limited. He'd just become another reason to feel the pull to come home. "How do you keep seeing parts of me naked?"

"How do you keep finding yourself naked and in situations where you need help?" he countered.

"I didn't need help this time."

"It sounded like you did."

"I think you wanted a peek."

He grinned. "If I wanted a peek, I would've turned around and watched. I only turned when you shrieked. So it's your fault I saw anything. However, if it's any consolation, what I saw, even fleetingly, was pretty spectacular."

She swallowed hard. She wouldn't let him know how much his comment rattled her. Not admitting her problem was definitely the first step to ignoring it.

They swam around in the pond together, but separately, and she had to admit it did feel good to rinse off. But now that her body temperature had dropped to a normal level again, the water felt almost too cold.

"How long do we need to stay in here exactly?" she asked.

"It's getting pretty chilly, isn't it?"

She nodded.

"Why don't we go see the lookout?"

Nibbling her lower lip, she hesitated to say yes. There

was one little problem. "I didn't bring a towel. What was the point of not swimming in our underwear if we have to turn around and put our clothes back on wet skin? This wasn't a good plan."

"True, but I've got an idea." He started to wade out of the water.

"Whoa there, big guy," she said, raising her hands to make him stop walking. He didn't.

"You noticed." He chuckled.

"You could warn me you're on the move. Don't you want me to turn away like before?"

"I never told you to turn away then either. I'm not afraid of you seeing me as I am, but if you'd feel better about it, then you better turn away now because this water isn't gonna cover me for much longer."

Oh sure. He's so confident. Doesn't care who sees what. Fine. If he doesn't want to cover up, then it's not my fault if I see—Whoa!

Water droplets rolled down Logan's back and shoulders, trailing along his skin until they crested the hills of his nicely sculpted ass. Forcing her eyes to the water around her, she refused to watch any longer.

The man was beyond attractive, no doubt, but that didn't mean she'd cave. And sure, he'd been nothing but sweet and kind and respectful to her the whole time she'd known him, but that still didn't mean she could give in to the temptation that was Logan. Not now. Not ever.

"You can come out now. I won't watch."

Tessa looked up to find Logan holding out a blanket in front of him like a wall. Where the blanket had come from she had no idea but she was immensely happy to see it. She could cover up and dry off without having to make her clothes damp.

She waded out of the water quickly, already shivering, and

pulled the blanket from his hands and wrapped it around her shoulders, crisscrossing the ends against her chest. Squatting down, she managed to grab her clothes and one strap of her backpack while still holding the edges of the blanket closed. When she stood, she finally took a second to look at Logan. He'd wrapped his shirt around his waist, and slung his backpack over one shoulder. The rest of his clothes hung from his hands down the front of him like a loincloth. His bare chest, close enough she could touch it, made her long to lick the water droplets from his skin as they ran in tiny rivers down his washboard abs.

"This way," she said, walking barefoot down the riverbank toward the lookout. She led them around a bend and past a thicket of trees and bushes that hid the lookout spot. "Be careful here since this isn't part of the path."

As she passed through the last overhang of tree cover, the lookout spot opened up into a small clearing right on the edge of the mountainside. There was no barrier between them and cliffs, just open, unobstructed views of the mountain range.

"Wow," Logan said, coming to stand beside her. "This view is stunning. Now I get why you hike all the way up here."

They stood side-by-side in silence for a few minutes enjoying the view. Tessa loved the way the sun beat down on the mountains, casting some of it into shadow while the rest practically glowed. The longer she looked, the more detail she saw, and she tried to commit every part of it to memory. When would she get to come up here again? Next summer? That felt like forever from now. But how soon did she want to come back to visit? Hadn't she tried too long to get away to already miss this place?

"I wish I'd thought to bring a blanket. Then we could have somewhere to sit down and relax for a while."

"We could use that blanket."

She shot him a sideways glance. "But then I'd be naked

again."

"True." He grinned. "And the problem would be?" His voice trailed off as he raised an eyebrow at her. "You keep the blanket, but I'm still going to lie out for a few minutes. I guess I'll lie on my shirt instead of letting it dry in the sun."

He's going to get naked and suntan?

Oh my...

She should not be excited about this situation. It was bad news for her keeping her distance from him. How could she hang out with him being naked and not want to jump his bones?

Because you're in control of your desires and you don't desire to get involved with him. He can sunbathe nude. It's totally natural.

He set his backpack in a patch of shade then nudged a few twigs out of the way as he cleared a spot to lie down. No matter how many sticks he moved, he'd still be sitting on the hard ground while she cuddled the soft blanket. The part of her brain wanting to keep her distance from Logan battled with the other part wanting to see him lying completely naked in the sun. Chiming in from the deepest recesses of her subconscious was the little voice of her inner sex kitten that *really* wanted an excuse to lie down naked beside him.

She'd known other people in high school who'd found little places in the mountains to skinny dip and sunbathe nude, but not here. This was her spot. One time, her ex-boyfriend Zack had wanted her to bring him here for some sexy time outdoors. Part of her had wanted to say yes, but for whatever reason she'd gone with her gut instinct and said no. And thank God she had. Who knows how many people would have found out about their adventure with his big mouth—probably the whole town would've known, as usual. A part of her always knew she couldn't trust him.

She didn't feel that same kind of hesitation in her gut

when it came to being here with Logan. This time instinct told her she could trust him with this secret place—with her body. In fact, the thought of being with him in this situation was too tempting to pass up.

People sunbathe nude in Europe all the time without ending up fooling around. We're friends. Lying in the sun. Like cats. But without the fur.

"Wait. You can have the blanket."

Shit! Why did I say that?

"What's that?" He stopped and turned to face her. His shirt was still tied around his waist and covered his groin.

Because I want to see what's under that shirt.

"You can use the blanket." She swallowed and prayed she was brave enough to deal with the repercussions of this moment in about a minute from now. "If you promise you will never tell a soul about this, especially not Travis."

"Are you saying you're going to get some sun too? Naked?" A grin slowly bloomed on his lips. His eyes seemed to light up as if they were reflecting the sun as well as his enthusiasm.

"Turn around," she said.

He laughed. "Why? You can't expect me to move around, literally on the edge of a cliff, with my eyes closed for the rest of the afternoon."

"Humor me. Please," she added, softly.

He turned his back.

If she'd thought it had been hard taking off her clothes and getting into the pond, this was at least triple the difficulty. Before she could talk herself out of it, she took off her blanket, shook it out, and arranged it on the flattest section of ground. Then she lay down on her stomach and rested her chin on her crossed arms, focusing on the beautiful view and slowing her heart rate, and *not* on the fact that she was laying in the sun, butt naked—literally—with an almost complete stranger. A sweet and dangerously sexy almost stranger.

"Okay. You can turn around."

She gritted her teeth together and fought the urge to roll up in the blanket like a human burrito. All he'd see was her butt and he'd already seen it once, he'd even touched it, so she needed to relax.

Tessa froze as Logan turned around.

"Nice," he whispered under his breath, but she still heard him loud and clear as if he'd yelled it from the mountaintop. Pride swelled within her at his understated compliment.

At the sound of a tiny groan coming from his direction, she almost glanced toward him. Instead, she forced herself to focus on nature.

An eagle flying in circles in the distance.

A songbird chirping in a near by tree.

Fluffy, white clouds gliding across the sky.

Logan's shirt falling to the ground. Oh shit.

The shirt that had been the only article of clothing covering his body.

He settled on the blanket beside her, close enough that she was ultra aware of his presence—she'd have to be dead not to notice him—but not close enough to accidentally touch each other. He'd chosen to lie on his back and fold his arms under his head as if he were casually reclining on the couch, not on a blanket in the middle of nature, naked…with a naked woman beside him.

Logan's penis is getting a suntan.

Don't do it… Don't do it…

"Do you have enough blanket?" she asked casually as she turned to look him in the eye.

But his eyes were closed against the bright sunlight. A lazy smile played on his lips. He looked so peaceful lying there. She was instantly glad she'd given up the blanket so they could both enjoy it.

The water that had been on his chest had long since dried and now his skin looked kissed by the sun's rays. She licked her lips. A faint dusting of hair on his chest grew thicker below his belly button, like a trail leading to—

Wowza. I said not to do that!

She could practically hear her inner sex kitten bouncing up and down with excitement and anticipation while her more rational, logical self cursed her for being weak and making things more difficult than they already were. If only she hadn't looked at what was hanging out, semi-erect, in the sunshine.

But it was too late. The damage was done. The package had been unwrapped.

Chapter Eleven

Tessa forced her gaze away from Logan's penis.

"Find something you like down there, sugar?"

The grin on his face told her everything she needed to know—she was busted. "Just making sure you're all good." She whipped her head back toward the view.

Just shut up.

"Everything up here is good, and I'm not talking about the view."

Getting naked to swim was definitely her first mistake. Agreeing to sunbathe nude was absolutely her second. Somehow she feared that if she looked at him again, she'd be well on her way to making her third mistake of the day. And yet, she looked at him anyway.

"I meant it looks like you have more than enough." She took a shaky breath. Why did her words keep coming out wrong? "Room. On the blanket."

"I've definitely got more than enough *room*. But if you're worried, I'll shift over." As he wiggled across the blanket an inch closer, she pressed her hand to his chest, stopping him.

"Don't," she said, locking her eyes with his. She wouldn't look anywhere but his face. But she didn't need to actually look at his chest to know how outstanding it was. She could feel it beneath her palm, under her trembling fingertips—firm, hot, muscular. Everything she'd guessed, but better.

He shook his head. "I haven't done anything. The only one doing anything is you, sugar."

"I haven't done anything either," she said, indignantly.

"No, not at all. But maybe you should tell that to your fingers because that thing your thumb is doing to my nipple is maddeningly arousing."

She glanced to her hand as if it was attached to someone else's body. Why was she fondling his body? The tiny beaded nub of his nipple was hard and she didn't have to wonder if other parts of his body were the same. She could see pretty well in her peripheral vision.

"I didn't mean to."

"I don't mind."

"I do." She tried to pull her hand back, but he covered hers with his, holding it against his skin.

"Why do you keep pulling away from me when you so obviously want something else? And don't give me your usual crap about the Dick you have back in the city, because we both know that's a scam."

She opened her mouth to make a smart-assed response. "I…"

What could she say? She was unbelievably attracted to him, both physically and mentally, but this wasn't an easy situation. If they'd met while he still lived in the city, maybe it would be. But he didn't, and it wasn't. She couldn't handle another connection pulling her back to Cutter's Creek.

"Because…" There was no way she could tell him the truth—that if they were in Central Park right now instead of on a mountain in West Virginia, she'd already be straddling his lap and screaming his name. She wouldn't have even tried to resist him.

She cleared her throat and tried to steady her nerves and stop thinking about how good it would feel to be with Logan. It wouldn't help either of them in the long run. It would only make transitions into their news lives more challenging. They both needed a clean slate to embrace their new surroundings—him in town and her in the city—didn't they? Having a fling now would complicate things later.

Logan's heartbeat drummed under her palm. He didn't have to tell her how he felt about her; she could read it all over his body language even if she hadn't been able to see his growing hard on.

"Why do you keep fighting this thing between us?" he asked, propping himself up on one elbow and moving even closer to her.

As soon as she figured out a way to get up without him seeing her boobs, she would get dressed and put a solid boundary of clothing between them. Naked sunbathing was a stupid idea.

He was right. She was fighting the chemistry between them and damn it, she feared she was about to lose the battle. "Because I'm not interested in you that way, okay?"

Logan let her hand go and laughed. "Right."

"What's that supposed to mean?"

"That you're full of shit."

She gasped. That was rude and uncalled for. "I am not. You asked for my reason and I gave it to you. I'm sorry if I hurt your precious ego, but that's my answer."

"You're a terrible liar. I know you do feel this thing between us, and I'm entirely sure you want to explore these feelings more, but you're stopping yourself. That's the part I can't figure out."

"Well, aren't you so sure of yourself. Egotistical much?"

"It's not egotistical to call you out on lying about your feelings when I've been open about mine." He motioned to where he still waited, semi-hard, looking all too eager to go the rest of the way.

Don't look again!

Against her will, her gaze fluttered down his body to the area in question.

"See, you're interested," he said, confidence filling his voice.

Damn it.

"And you're irritating," she retorted.

"Because I'm right. And I'm willing to admit what I want."

"Oh yeah, and what exactly do you want, Mr. I'm So Sure Of Everything?"

"The same thing I've wanted since Travis first mentioned his girlfriend's annoying little sister and told me about you. The same thing I've wanted since the moment I almost ran you off the road by accident. The same thing I've wanted since I saved you from that spider—I want you, Tessa.

"I want to know why you hate it here so much when you have a family that loves you. I want to know what you think about living in the city. What it felt like to move there. I want to know how you can draw such amazing pictures yet still think you aren't talented."

"Really? You want to know that stuff about me?" He wasn't only looking to get laid?

"Yep. And about a million other things I've wanted to ask you about in the last few days, but haven't since you're also so…"

She narrowed her eyes. "So what?"

"So bitchy sometimes."

She smacked his chest and the slapping noise echoed around them, accentuating her statement. "I am not."

"You are, but that's okay because at least when you're bitchy with me it means you're talking to me. And slowly but surely I'm winning you over."

"What do you mean, you're winning me over? I'm not a prize to be won."

"I mean I've got you here, alone, in the woods, on a gorgeous sunshine-filled day, naked. And instead of being bitchy with me as usual, you can't keep your hands off me. You want to be here with me, like this, in this moment, even if you don't want to admit it."

His gaze was so intense her breath caught in her lungs, and it was as if she was underwater, fighting to get to the surface for air. His gaze hadn't left her eyes once, and every part of her body begged for his attention.

"Ask me again what I want," he said so softly she found herself leaning in to hear him.

"What do you want, Logan?" she asked, biting her lip with anticipation.

"You. Right here. Right now. All of you." His fingertips stroked the back of her hand where it still rested on his chest. "And I want you to want me just as badly."

She did. She'd been trying to ignore it, to fight it, but damn it, she wanted Logan. When she'd made the decision to skinny dip, she knew exactly what she was doing and why. As much as she needed to, she couldn't stay away from him. Even though she knew getting involved with him had the potential to leave her hurt, she couldn't stop herself.

"I…" She paused.

"What do you want, sugar?" he asked, wrapping his hand around the nape of her neck and lacing his fingers into her hair.

"You," she whispered.

"It's about fucking time you said it out loud." He grinned and then pulled her face to his. His mouth pressed to hers and with a gasp of pure pleasure, her lips parted. He took advantage of the moment and swept his tongue across her lips before plunging inside.

Without breaking their kiss, she inched across the blanket to snuggle into his side, melting into him. The heat of their bodies together and the heat of the sun beating down combined to create an inferno around them. When the breeze blew up from the cliff, it brushed across her hot skin and left a cooling wake, making her skin tingle.

Logan's hand snaked down her spine to settle on her ass. He caressed it and squeezed gently. With a groan, he did it again, harder. "I've been dreaming of touching you again since that moment in the cabin," he said.

"I hope it lived up to your expectations."

He shrugged. "Meh." It wasn't even a word, just a sound of ambivalence.

"Meh?" she questioned. "You've been dreaming about touching my ass and now it's simply okay? I have a great ass. What's wrong with my ass?" She tried to roll away, back to her side of the blanket where she obviously should've stayed.

His arms locked around and he grinned. Chuckling, he said, "I was only kidding."

"Well, it wasn't funny."

He dragged her leg over to drape across his. The skin of her thigh tingled as he slid his hand up to her ass, caressing and kneading along the way. "It's better than I remember. You have an amazing ass." He smacked it and any hint of teasing disappeared from his expression, replaced instead by pure lust.

She kissed him, hard. Everything around them quieted. There were no birds singing in the trees, no breeze blowing through the branches, no waterfall in the distance. Instead there was only the sound of his breath mixing with hers, the slight whisper of his hands moving on her skin, the pounding of her pulse in her ears.

Tessa kissed his jaw and neck on the way to his chest. She

paused for a brief moment to take in the gorgeous scenery of his chest and abdomen. "I don't usually care about physical looks, but damn, you're hot. Your pecs are like…movie star pecs. They should be famous."

"I'll have to find them an agent."

She giggled. "I know you put a lot of time and effort into your body because it's your business, and I have to say, job well done. You deserve a raise."

He laughed. "Thanks. I work out because it's my job and because I love it. It makes me feel good."

She swirled her tongue across his nipple and he groaned. "But this feels even better."

"I'm showing appreciation for all your hard work."

"Anywhere else you feel like bestowing your appreciation is fine with me," he said, twining his fingers in her hair as she kissed his chest, then ribs, then belly button.

By the time she got to his waist she was greeted by his fully erect and patiently waiting for her penis. She'd thought it had looked impressive before with her quick glimpses of it, but seeing it up close… *Wow.*

If personal training didn't work out, the man should work for UPS because he knew how to carry a package. She rubbed her fingertips from tip to base, enjoying his quick intake of breath as she did. When she wrapped her hand around him and alternated between stroking and squeezing, he groaned loudly. Flicking her tongue across the tip, she paused to glance up at him. His eyes were intensely focused on her as he watched every movement. When she tasted him again, encompassing him fully with her lips, he shuddered beneath her. His eyelids fluttered closed and his head flopped back onto the blanket.

Knowing she was the source of his pleasure made her want him even more. She moved her hand and mouth in a slowly increasing pace, enjoying every second. By the time he rolled her onto her back, she was trembling with her own unmet need and desire.

He hovered over her, pinning her hands to the ground above her head, making her breasts jut up toward him. She felt alive and free and more uninhibited than she ever had before. Maybe it was the fresh air and sunshine on her naked body. Or maybe it was Logan who brought out this feeling in her, made her come out of her protective shell both figuratively and literally. Whatever it was, she hadn't felt this way before, and she never wanted it to end.

"Are you going to stare at me or kiss me?" she asked.

"I feel like I've been waiting forever to see you like this… to have you like this. I plan on taking my time while I kiss every inch of your body."

A tremble of excitement rippled through her.

"And I'm starting right here." He sucked one of her taut nipples into his mouth. His tongue rolled around the tight bud, then his teeth gently bit down on it. She gasped and arched into him, both wanting more and wanting him to stop at the same time. The pleasure was too good. She wanted him to do it again and as if reading her mind, he did. Every scrape of his teeth and sweep of his tongue on her skin made her want him to touch her and taste her everywhere.

He slid down her stomach and nudged her thighs apart. When his lips pressed to her most sensitive skin, she feared she might crumble apart with the shockwaves he sent coursing through her body. She moaned and grabbed his shoulders, needing something tangible to hold onto since the world had to be coming apart beneath her. With every lap of his tongue, he brought her closer and closer to the point of total bliss until she felt like she was falling off the cliff behind her. The world spun around her as he kissed his way back up her stomach to her breasts.

"That was… You were…" She tried but failed to find

adequate words. "Get a... So we can..." Surely he had to know what she was saying.

"Hold on. I think I have one in my backpack," he said, giving her nipple one last kiss before crawling away from her.

She propped herself up on her elbow, watching him, her head feeling less foggy. "What do you mean you think you have one? You're a guy. You always have one, don't you?"

"Well, that's sexist," he said, unzipping the compartments on his bag and tossing the contents to the dirt.

"But also true. Right?"

"Well, if we were at my place, I'd have an endless supply of them, of course. In fact, I'd have a big dish full of them right at the front door to give out as welcome gifts to women who decide to stop by my apartment."

"Shut up. You know what I mean."

"Ah ha!" he cheered, crawling back with his found treasure between his teeth. He dropped it onto her belly and grinned. "I do know what you mean. But no, I don't always have one on me. Silly me, I thought most women would call me egotistical if I presumed that they might want to sleep with me and brought along provisions wherever I went."

"Oh we would." She picked up the foil packet and toyed with the edge, debating if she should tear it open or not. They couldn't go any further if she didn't. "So you presumed you'd get lucky with me today, did you?"

He took the packet from her fingers and tore it open, then rolled it onto his length. She couldn't help but watch. And squirm with anticipation. His pre-show had been outstanding, but she bet his main event would be even more fantastic.

"I didn't presume anything, but I'd have to be an idiot not to be prepared in any situation. That's why my emergency first aid kit has one of these bad boys in it." He tossed the foil to the side and crawled between her legs, pausing at her entrance while he pulled her legs around his waist.

"In case of emergency hard on, tear foil. That kind of thing?" She practically vibrated while waiting impatiently for him to slide into her heat.

"Yep," he said simply. He leaned forward and kissed her, taking his time to explore her mouth as he inched into her, achingly slow. Her heat surrounded his length until she felt like she couldn't take him any further. "I didn't presume, but I might have hoped like hell."

With that he withdrew and quickly thrust into her again and again. He reached so deep her head spun. She thrust with him, intensifying each movement. Her nails scratched down his back as she called out his name. He felt so good, so right.

"Stop. Roll over," she said, between panting for breaths.

He did as she asked, taking her with him. When she settled onto his lap, straddling him, she rocked back and forth. He thrust upward. She made sounds she'd never heard herself make before—primal, guttural, deeply satisfied sounds.

Closing her eyes, she arched back and raised her face to the sky. The sunlight kissed every spot of her body, heating it, while the breeze simultaneously cooled her. She'd never felt more at peace with her life. For once she wasn't running from the past or searching for her future. She was simply in the moment with Logan.

He grabbed her hips and drove hard and deep, forcing her to take more of him. She swiveled her hips, drawing him in, holding him hostage. Her body suddenly clenched around him as another wave of ecstasy overwhelmed her. He called out her name with his release and his hands fell to the blanket. She waited for her head to stop spinning before moving to curl into his side, her head resting on his chest.

This was what life was supposed to feel like—free, happy, weightless.

She didn't know how, but she hoped there was some way to hold on to this feeling forever.

Chapter Twelve

"This is nice." Logan sighed loudly, contentedly.

"What is?"

"This. Today. Being out in the fresh air. Being here with you. All of it."

"It is." And she meant it more than she thought she would before making the hike. Being up here again reminded her about why she'd longed to see the rest of the world to begin with. This view inspired her to see more.

Being here with Logan, she felt not only inspired by the view but also by the incredible man beside her. He relaxed on the blanket while she sketched and felt calmer than she had in months. Whether it was from being on vacation, or from being with Logan, she didn't know. But she liked the feeling and she didn't want it end. She wanted to capture it forever in her sketchbook so one day she could look back on today and remember this feeling of serenity.

"When Travis mentioned there was a job available here and that he might be able to help me get it, I was pretty desperate for the work. I didn't want to be a trainer at someone else's gym, and being a private personal trainer is difficult to get started and be successful at. Once New Yorkers find a person they like and who works with their schedule, they're loyal. It's great when you're the one secure in your job, but it's frustrating when you're the new guy."

"I know that feeling." Every gallery she'd gone to in the city already had their core artists. It didn't matter that her work fell in line with the style of art they were already showcasing, they simply wouldn't give her a chance.

She checked her cell phone for a signal. Nothing. She thought it wouldn't be a problem to get one up on the mountaintop, but it was, which meant she hadn't gotten her emails all day. Of course, a break from them was probably a good thing. Every time she'd gotten a reply from a gallery, it had been a rejection. Only one hadn't responded yet and all her hopes were pinned on it.

"Having trouble getting your foot in the door too?" he asked.

"You could say that."

"If the work you're showing them is anything like the sketch I saw the other day, then they're the ones missing out. Your work is incredible."

"Tell that to my empty bank account." She smiled weakly.

His compliments were appreciated, but it made her wish that even one of the galleries or studios felt the same. Of course, he'd seen one of the sketches she'd done here, which was completely different than the work she was showing in the city. But all of it was still done by her hand and with her eye for style, light, angle, and detail.

The work she'd shown in the city was new, exciting, and fresh.

She'd done a million sketches of the trees and mountains and lakes. When she'd moved to the city, she'd wanted to try something different so she'd painted the city on her canvases instead. Getting the angles and colors right had been challenging at first, but she was having fun and liked the way her paintings turned out. Too bad no one else did.

"Thanks." She didn't want to talk about that stuff right now. Her current situation in the city made her feel like a failure. She didn't want to feel that today. "Want to see this one?"

Normally, she kept her sketchbook private to everyone, her family included. But Logan had already seen one and liked it, and since this one was about today, maybe he'd like it too. She'd been completely bared to him physically so showing him a sketch couldn't make her feel anymore exposed.

"Definitely," he said, rolling onto his side toward her. Thankfully, they'd put on their underwear after fooling around or else she would've gotten another eyeful. Not that she would've minded the view, but it would've made her want to be with him again. And she wasn't sure if she wanted that or not.

He'd been amazing, outstanding actually, but being with him again would only deepen her feelings and make things harder for her at the end of the week. Of course, looking at his chest made her want to touch it and kiss it and all her logic started seeping out her ears. Good thing he'd only had one condom, which meant there was zero chance of them getting busy again.

She handed him her book and held her breath while he looked over the sketch of himself, lying on the blanket. Instantly, she wished she could grab it back and erase it from his memory. It wasn't good enough. That line needed to be smoothed and the arch of his eyebrow wasn't right. Not to mention the angle of his knee was off by at least a couple of degrees, and she couldn't even look at the shadows on the ground. Those were all wrong.

"This is incredible. You did this today?"

She nodded. "I know there's a lot to be fixed."

"Sugar, this is perfect. I love it." His voice sounded genuine. She mumbled her thanks and took the book back, closing it quickly so she wouldn't have to look at it anymore.

"Were you sad to leave the city when you got the job here?" She couldn't imagine going from having everything you could ever desire at your fingertips to being here, where there was nothing but nature for miles.

"No, I was excited. I couldn't wait to get out of the noise and congestion. Of course, I never knew it would be this rural, but I don't mind. I love the quiet. I love being able to come to a place like this and not see a single building."

"But don't you find it boring after all the excitement there is in the city?"

"No. I grew up with that excitement and after a while it becomes noise. I never felt like I could be alone, even in my apartment. Here, it's completely different. The first night I stayed in my new place I couldn't believe how noisy the critters were and how I didn't hear a single person or vehicle."

"I like the hustle and bustle of the city. Always having so many people around that no one even takes notice of who you are or what you're doing. I finally feel like I can be whoever I want to be and not who people expect me to be. I can run to the coffee shop in my slippers and it won't be the talk of the town the next day. It's awesome."

"You go to the coffee shop in your slippers often?" he asked, smirking.

"Never. But the point is, I could, and that is a freedom I never got here." She grabbed a granola bar from her bag and took a bite and washed it down with a sip of water. "I'm warning you, this town will know everything about you and they'll tell everyone they know. Before you know it, you'll wish for the anonymous life in the city again."

"I was no one in the city my whole life. I didn't even know

my neighbors' names after living beside them for years. Here, people already say hello to me by name when I walk into the coffee shop. They ask me if I'm settled, if I need anything. It's nice to feel cared about."

"Oh they care alright—about your hair, and your new ball cap and the book you're reading and how often you buy toilet paper. No thanks."

"Is that why you're so insistent about not living here? Because people care about you too much?"

When he said it like that it sounded stupid, but it was more than that. "It's because I'm tired of everyone having a say in how I live my life. It's about knowing there is more to life than this little town and the people in it. I want to see the world."

"Can't you go on vacations like everyone else?" he asked.

"Can't you mind your own business? Oh, wait, nope, you live in Cutter's Creek now. I guess that means you'll start hounding me to stay here too."

She flopped back onto the blanket, thankful that the sun was behind the trees so she could watch the clouds floating by without getting blinded. Why did he have to be like the rest of them, bugging her about her choices? Why couldn't he accept her for who she was and what she wanted?

"I obviously hit a sensitive spot and not in the good way like earlier either." He laughed as if he'd made a joke, but she didn't laugh. "I'm sorry. I didn't mean to get into your business. I was only making conversation and trying to figure you out."

The silence between them was suddenly thick with tension. She sighed. "I'm sorry too. The whole issue is a bit of a sore spot for me."

"I know you have reasons for making your choices, but I wish I understood them." He shrugged. "If I had a family like yours, I'd do whatever it took to stay nearby."

"I guess we want different things in life."

They did want different things in life—he wanted small town community; she wanted big city anonymity. He wanted to settle in and start a business; she wanted to be recognized for her paintings, and not because she was a Cutter in Cutter's Creek. Their situations were like oil and water. Unmixable.

From now on, she needed to keep that in mind. Sleeping with Logan was a fun distraction from real life, but she wasn't about to let it change the path she walked toward her future.

L ogan yawned as he grabbed himself a beer from the small cooler tucked between the lawn chairs. It was only mid-afternoon, but he'd already worked out, hiked up a mountain, had mind-blowing sex with Tessa, and hiked back down the mountain. Honestly, he deserved a nap. But he'd hardly hung out with Travis and the idea of lounging on the dock with a fishing pole was too good to pass up.

"Heard you and Tessa went up to the lookout. Alone." Travis had that tone in his voice, the one that said he was fishing for more than bass.

"Mary was supposed to join us but I guess she had to do something with James."

"I noticed you both came back from hiking so you obviously started getting along better. I was worried she might toss you off the cliff if you kept annoying her."

"We got along great." That sounded way too enthusiastic. He might have hooked up with Tessa, but that didn't mean he wanted to tell his buddy about it yet. "Well, better than before. I think she's finally over the accident and hating me."

"Sounds like a lot of effort for little pay off. That isn't an easy hike."

"Have you seen the view from up there? That alone was worth the trip."

"What else was worth the trip? Time with Tessa?"

Logan shrugged. He might not want to share all the details with Travis, and he had promised to keep Tessa's secret about her fake Dick in the city, but that didn't mean he couldn't admit to enjoying the view of more than nature up on the mountain. "That part was good too."

Travis cast his line. "I always thought you'd hit it off with her. I was surprised to see you butting heads, but I guess I shouldn't have been since that's the way Tessa communicates with everyone. It's like she's always on edge and defensive. I wish she'd chill out."

A prickle of annoyance took root. "Maybe if she didn't have you guys always on her case she'd be able to."

Travis shot him a look that was both amused and confused. "You need a tampon to go with that mood swing?"

Logan took a long gulp of his beer finishing it off. "Sorry," he finally said as he grabbed a fresh one from the cooler. "Tessa mentioned how much the family wants her to move back and how she wants to try things on her own in the city for awhile. I guess I'm kind of on her side."

"Did she bitch about us the whole time?"

"No. And I wouldn't say she bitched about it either. We just talked."

"Sounds like you did too much talking, in my opinion."

Logan thought about their time together on the mountain—being inside Tessa, her nails raking down his back, having her call out his name while he pounded balls deep into her heat. "We didn't talk the whole time."

"What else is there to do? Bird watching?"

"Skinny dipping."

Travis turned, a huge smile on his face. "Are you telling me you saw my sister-in-law swimming naked?"

"We were simply sharing a water source to cool off. And no, I didn't see her swimming naked."

When I saw her naked, she was about to have her way with me on the blanket, not swimming. Totally different question than Travis asked, so therefore, not a lie.

"Sounds like a missed opportunity, if you ask me."

"No one's asking you anything, and it wasn't a missed opportunity. It was gentlemanly. Not all of us are looking to get laid all the time."

Though I did. And it was awesome.

"Most of us are." Travis laughed. "Well, whatever you did or didn't do, I'm glad you're hitting it off with Tessa. She needs someone to keep her in line, and I always thought you'd be a good fit for her."

"You remember she has a boyfriend, right?" He swallowed his annoyance at having to keep her lie. He didn't want to pretend there was a guy she cared about, who got to sleep with her on a regular basis. The thought of someone taking up the role of her boyfriend irritated him. "I'm not here to date her."

"No, no…of course you aren't, but I've known both of you for so long, I've always imagined you guys getting along."

"You make it sound like we're meant to be together, like you're setting us up or something."

Travis downed the rest of his beer and looked out to the water. It wasn't like his friend to be evasive.

"This isn't a set up, is it?" Logan asked.

Travis opened his mouth to speak and the glint in his eyes triggered suspicion inside Logan. Before his friend could confirm or deny the question, Martha walked up and interrupted them.

"Hi, boys."

"Martha," they both said in unison.

"Listen, I know I mentioned it briefly before, but everyone here takes a turn cooking. Tomorrow morning you and Tessa are on breakfast duty. She's already agreed to it so I hope you don't mind."

"Not at all. I'm sure I can find something to whip up. Although, I might need my blender from my apartment."

"That shouldn't be a problem. Tessa's going into town to get the things she needs so you can go with her. I think she's heading out in a few minutes."

Logan reeled in his hook and set the rod on the dock. "I'll catch up with you later to finish this conversation."

"Better go get Tessa before you miss her."

The words were simple enough, but Logan couldn't help but feel his friend had meant to say them with a double meaning.

Chapter Thirteen

Logan lounged back against the passenger seat while Tessa drove the winding road into town. They only had an hour for the trip before they'd be late for dinner, but since town was only ten minutes from their campsite, he didn't think they'd have to rush too much.

"So what are our breakfast plans for tomorrow?" he asked. "I'm not much of a cook, but I can scramble some eggs. And of course I'll make my famous green smoothies."

"Good luck with that."

"With what?"

"The green smoothies. My family won't drink those. They might eat green vegetables, but they certainly won't drink them." She sounded so matter-of-fact about it that it annoyed him.

"Why wouldn't they? They're delicious and filled with stuff that's good for you."

"And kale."

He scoffed. "I don't have to put kale in. I could use spinach instead."

She giggled. "'Cause that would be so much better?"

"Yes, it would. It has less bitterness and is still healthy."

"I'll take your word for it, but you should take my word and believe me when I tell you not to waste your money buying lots of smoothie supplies. My family will eat my breakfast, not your healthy drink."

"Oh yeah?" he asked. If he could convince them to taste it, he knew they would love them. "I bet someone in the Cutter family drinks my green beast smoothie."

"You're on. Get ready to lose."

"What're you making anyway?"

"Crepes with strawberries, bananas, and a hazelnut chocolate spread."

His mouth watered. It sounded decadent. Way more luxurious and extravagant than he usually ate for breakfast. And imagining Tessa licking chocolate sauce from her lips was almost enough to make him hard again. He couldn't wait to devour her culinary masterpiece. But he also couldn't admit that, not when she gave him a hard time about his smoothie, which now knowing the other breakfast options would never be the top choice by her family. She'd made a smart bet. He was definitely the long shot in this breakfast duel.

"Sounds delicious. And fattening."

She narrowed her eyes but didn't take them off the road to glare at him. "The fruit is healthy."

"Everything else isn't."

"Well, you don't have to have any. Of course, once you smell my crepes you'll be begging for a taste."

He'd beg for another taste of her. The way she constantly stood her ground turned him on. "You want me to beg for a taste?" he asked, his voice low. He squeezed her thigh. "I thoroughly enjoyed the taste I had of you earlier. Tonight I'd happily beg for more, if that's what it takes to get you again."

A deep pink hue bloomed on the apples of her cheeks.

"That was a one time thing. I thought you understood that I can't let my family find out what happened between us or they'll know I don't have a guy back in the city."

"I wasn't planning on inviting them back to the cabin. Of course, you may need to be a little quieter this time around. You'll have to bite a pillow or something while I do that thing with my tongue that you liked so much."

"I don't know what you're talking about, but I'm sure it won't happen again. I'm not giving them any more reason to pressure me into staying."

He slid his hand up her thigh until he couldn't go any further, then gently pressed his fingers against her, making a circular motion. She gasped and her knuckles turned white on the steering wheel. "Still don't remember?"

"Stop it," she said, removing his hand from her body. Her voice was stern but she smiled despite the words. She wanted him too, even if she didn't want to admit it. "I'm driving. One accident this week is enough."

Tessa slowed the truck as they drove into town. They turned onto Main Street and he peered out the windows at the small buildings passing by. "For such a small town, I still haven't learned where everything is."

"You'll figure it out soon enough. It's not like you can get lost." She pulled into May's Grocery and found a parking spot. Tessa glanced at the clock on the dashboard. "We better hurry. She closes up at about five thirty."

That gave them ten minutes to get their shopping done. "What happens when you need something later?" He hadn't run into that situation yet, but it was only a matter of time until he ran out of toilet paper or some other necessity after May's store closed for the day.

"Then you hope the gas station on the highway has what you need. The drugstore down the block stays open until ten most nights."

"Good to know there's options," he said, pulling open the door to the grocery store and held it open for Tessa. His hand naturally went to her lower back as she passed.

"Barely. One of the things I love about the city is I can get anything I need at any time, day or night."

"I'll give you that. The city never sleeps."

"Sometimes this place feels like it's in a coma."

They went their separate ways inside the store and quickly grabbed the supplies they needed for breakfast. When they got back out to the truck, Tessa opened the cooler her dad kept in the back and placed the food inside on top of a fresh few bags of ice they'd also bought.

"I need to run down to the drug store for a few things. You need anything?" she asked.

He did need something…well, wanted something. He'd hoped to find a set of oil pastels for Tessa as a small gift. He'd once seen this artist who did all their work with them and the pictures were some of the most beautiful he'd ever seen. He already thought her work was fantastic and could only imagine what they might look like with the new medium.

"I have another stop I want to make. I'll meet you back here in a few minutes."

She nodded and wandered off toward the drugstore while he turned and headed in the opposite direction to the hobby shop. The aisles were filled with wood working projects, sewing supplies, paints and every other hobby he could imagine. And yet every aisle he checked seemed to be lacking the one thing he wanted.

At the back of the store a guy who looked about his age was sanding a length of wood. By the look of the attention to detail the guy was giving it, it would be a beautiful picture frame when it was finished.

"Can I help you?" the guy asked, looking up from his work.

"If you could point me in the right direction to find the oil pastels, that would be great."

"This way," he said, coming into the main store. Logan followed behind wondering where he'd missed them since he'd looked everywhere. "You one of the artists who like to hang out at Granite Knolls Lake?"

He shook his head. "They're a gift. I'm not an artist."

"Oh? What brings you to town then?"

"I'm Logan Ridley, the new gym teacher. I'm filling in while the other one is on maternity leave. But I'd like to stay longer if I can. It seems like a nice town."

"Nice to meet you. Zack Maxwell," he said, shaking Logan's proffered hand. "You like baseball? Football?"

"I'm more of a hockey fan myself, but I don't mind watching the others too. You?"

"I watch them all. Hey, if you're around, a couple of guys and me get together at the bar to watch the games on the big screen. You want to join us next week?"

Logan nodded. He needed to make friends with more than the Cutter family if he wanted to settle in. "Sounds good."

"Great." Zack smiled and pointed to a spot on the shelf Logan must have walked by twice. "Here's what we got for pastels. Not a huge selection, but I don't get much demand for them. If you find something you like, Cheryl will ring you in at the front. If there's something you want me to order in specifically, let me know."

"Thanks. For the supplies and the invite. I'll see you next week."

As Zack wandered away, Logan surveyed the oil pastels options. Selecting one with a good variety of colors that included a convenient case, he made his purchase and walked back to meet Tessa at the truck. When he didn't see her there, he pulled down the back tailgate and jumped up to sit on the truck bed and people watch while he waited. Only there were no people out on the street to watch. Not quite the crowd hurrying down Fifth Avenue he was used to, but he didn't mind the quiet either.

Tessa peered self-consciously at the boxes of blues and purples and blacks in front of her and glanced down the aisle to make sure no one was watching. Why had she even stopped here? It wasn't like she needed any of these anyway. They'd simply caught her eye. It wasn't as if she was actually contemplating buying any of them.

Extra large? *Ouch.*

Extra small? *Definitely not.*

Lubricated? *Did anyone want it dry?*

Nope. Not happening!

She did not need to buy condoms. Sure, every girl should have a few handy, just in case. But she'd already had her "just in case" moment with Logan and she wasn't planning on having another anytime soon.

She wandered the rows of cosmetics deciding if she needed a new lipstick or if she wanted one to impress Logan, which was stupid because she was purposefully trying *not* to lead him on. She didn't want to be involved with him. Well, not again, at least.

The first time, this morning — *Was it only this morning?* — felt like so long ago she was already craving him again. But not so long ago that she'd forgotten the touch of his hands on her body, or his tongue on her skin, or…

Nope. Moving on. Think of something else.

Lip balm. She'd get that instead. It was practical and didn't mean that she was hoping to attract his attention.

Or tinted lip balm.

That was even better. Everyone could use a hint of color,

but it was still practical. Sure. She put the item in her basket along with the travel-sized hand lotion, hair clips, and tissue, then found herself wandering past the row of brightly colored boxes again.

Twelve pack.

Twenty-four pack.

Sixty-four pack? *Wow. Someone gets a lot or plans to. You will not buy these. You will not have sex with Logan again.*

Her cheeks burned as she scurried away from the embarrassing boxes and down another row, grabbing items at random and putting them in her basket. Her mind was too foggy with indecision to think clearly. She couldn't let herself give in and sleep with Logan again. The first time had been too good. She already liked him way more than she wanted to. She couldn't handle falling for him totally, and buying condoms was definitely agreeing to be with him again, which would lead to her falling even harder for him.

So no. She couldn't buy condoms. She wouldn't.

Tessa stopped at the end of the aisle, the boxes in question taunting her. She'd come in here to get lotion because the sun was making her skin dry, and she already had some in her basket. She didn't actually need to purchase anything else. And yet, those boxes called to her, begged her to grab one.

It's important to be prepared…

They last a long time…

I'll need them in the city when I eventually meet someone else I want to start a relationship with. So, okay then. She wandered closer. Chewing her lip, she read the packages again.

Ribbed? *Eww. Why?*

Ultra thin? *Don't I want ultra thick for ultra safety?*

"Glow in the dark? What the hell? Who's buying these things?" she whispered to herself.

"Need any help?" a voice asked beside her.

Her head whipped to the side so quickly the muscle pinched. "Nope. I was looking for this!" She spun around to put the condoms behind her and reached blindly for whatever was on the opposite shelf and grabbed a container. "Here it is."

She held it up triumphantly with a smile. Daniel Parker was smiling back at her. She'd had a crush on him in tenth grade. He'd never even given her the time of day. And now he'd caught her looking at condoms. Great.

"Tessa? Hey. I didn't know you were in town," Daniel said.

"Yep, back for the week. Heading out again in a couple of days."

A voice came over the intercom speaker. "Daniel to the pharmacy for customer assistance."

"I guess I have to run. Maybe I'll see you around. Let me know if you need any instruction on how to use that. It's what I'm here for."

"Will do! Bye!" she called overly cheerfully as he hurried away.

Looking down at the container, her head spun as if she'd been hit with a two-by-four. Vaginal itch cream. Great. Exactly the rumor she needed floating around town.

Shoving it onto the shelf, she spun back around and grabbed the first box of condoms she found—large, lubricated, and not glow in the dark. Good enough. With cheeks glowing so hot with embarrassment she could probably spark a match with them, she walked straight for the checkout. The sooner she was out of here, the better.

She sighed with relief when she saw the person at the register was some younger kid she didn't know. The last thing she needed was to run into anyone while buying condoms. As if itch cream was any better.

"Did you find everything you were looking for?" the

checkout girl asked.

"Yes." She fished out her debit card and was ready to swipe it at the first chance she got when her gaze felt to the items currently being rung through from her basket.

Lip balm. Steel wool scrubber.

What the hell did I pick up? Her heart pounded. Condoms would look mighty weird with this lot of goods.

Hand lotion. Condoms. Tissue. Rubber gloves. Hair clips.

She rolled her eyes and said a silent prayer for this moment to end. Or never have existed in the first place.

The girl took the basket from the counter and was tucking it away to make room for the bag. "Oh. Almost forgot this one." She scanned it quickly before dropping it into the bag, but not before Tessa noticed the smirk on her face.

Constipation medicine. *Awesome.*

Tessa swiped her card quickly, punched in her code, took her bag and receipt, and scurried out the door. She took a deep breath, trying to convince herself that by morning the whole town wouldn't know that she was getting laid, cleaning something dirty, had dry skin, and couldn't poop without medicinal assistance.

"Can you stop by my apartment before we head out?" Logan asked.

He heard about the condoms already!

"Why? What do you need? I'm not going to sleep with you again."

"Um, okay. Good to know. And random." He chuckled. "I need to grab my blender so I can make smoothies tomorrow."

The breath she hadn't realized she was holding came out in a puff. "Sure. Yeah. Where's your place?"

"The building on Third."

She didn't need any more information than that. There were only two apartment buildings in town—one on Third and the other on Seventh. Neither was all that great, but as a temporary place to stay they weren't terrible either. She'd definitely seen worse apartments in the city. Hell, she lived in a worse place in the city.

"Want to come in?"

Yes.

"No. We should go. Dinner will be ready soon and everyone will be looking for us."

He nodded and opened the door, taking a small bag with him. "I'll be right back."

While she waited, Tessa flipped on the radio and turned it up when a good song came on. It wasn't often she heard country music anymore. Seemed it wasn't the popular choice in the city. But there was something about the twang-y tune that comforted her like a warm blanket on a cold night. Before the song ended, Logan was back with a duffle bag.

"That's a blender?" she asked, pulling onto the street.

"And a couple of other things I needed."

Tessa got back onto the highway and headed toward the campground. The silence between them was comfortable as they drove until Logan asked her a question she didn't want to answer.

"What happened that made you so set on leaving this town? I know it's not my business, but you seem to fit in here and everyone is nice. And it's beautiful, quiet, and clean. I can't imagine wanting to leave it so desperately."

"Why do you want to know so bad?" she asked.

"If I'm keeping your fake boyfriend a secret, I deserve to know why you made one up in the first place."

Did she want to tell him? Did she want to dredge up the past and let another person know about her personal life when she didn't need to? "Does it matter?" she asked instead.

"Yes and no." He was quiet for a few breaths, looking out the window at the passing trees and boulders. "I guess it doesn't matter if you feel strongly about not telling me. I only asked because I want to know more about you, Tessa. I wasn't lying earlier when I said I wanted to know everything about you. I wasn't trying to get you into bed."

"It wasn't one single incident that made me want to leave. It was a combination of things that added up over time. I like being myself even when I go against the grain. But it's hard to do in a little town where everyone gossips all the time."

"Can't you ignore them?"

Maybe someone else could, but she couldn't. As a Cutter, she never got to fly under the radar. Her family had helped to establish the town more than a hundred years ago. She didn't think it was important, but everyone else did.

"I tried to let the comments and rumors and whispers roll off my shoulders like they didn't bother me. Most of the time I was pretty good. I got really good at hiding what I was doing or with who. Not because I did anything bad, but because I didn't want everyone else's thoughts about it later on."

"What pushed you over the edge and made you leave?"

Was it such a big deal? No. Sure, it would always be a part of her history and a contributing factor to who she was today, but it didn't define her. It was a stupid thing from her past. Besides, he'd hear it mentioned around town eventually anyway since she couldn't trust the town to keep her history in the past where it belonged. He may as well hear it from her.

"I had a boyfriend when I left for college. He stayed here and kept working while I went to school. I thought he was the one." She cleared her throat, not because she was getting choked up, but because she'd never had to tell anyone the story before. Everyone in Cutter's Creek knew. "I came home for summer break, and he'd gotten me a job at the card shop. He kept telling me how great an opportunity it was. I worked the stupid job to make him happy and I started to overhear the gossip from customers coming in. One particular story about a guy cheating on his unsuspecting girlfriend while she was away at school captured my attention. Can you imagine my surprise when I learned I was the girlfriend being cheated on?"

"I'm sorry, Tessa. I can't believe anyone would cheat on you."

"I think that part sucks, of course. But the part that drives me crazy is the whole town knew it was happening before I did and no one told me until I accidentally found out."

"That's what made you want to leave." He said it as a statement, not a question. "Now I get it."

Finally, someone else understands me.

Chapter Fourteen

There was enough time for an early morning jog and shower before Logan had to be in the main cabin with Tessa making breakfast. When he sat on the bed to tie his sneakers, she groaned.

"Why are you up? It's too early," she mumbled.

Her hair was splayed out on the pillow making her look a little like Medusa, not that he'd ever say that out loud. He didn't have a death wish. She stretched and rolled toward his bed, her breasts lolling gently to the side under her shirt. Damn, he'd like to see them again, up close.

He'd take them bouncing in a sports bra too. "I'm going for a jog before breakfast. Come with me."

"Why would I want to do that when I could stay here and do this?" She pulled her blanket over her head.

"Because it's a beautiful day out, and you should get some exercise."

"I hiked up a mountain yesterday. I did my exercise for the month."

He grinned. She didn't need to exercise anymore than he

did, but he wanted her company and knew the only way to get it was to trick her into coming. His way might be unorthodox, but it'd hopefully get the job done. "I didn't realize you were so out of shape. I guess it's better that you stay since you'd probably slow me down."

The blanket flipped off her and Tessa sat up, glaring at him. "Did you just call me fat?"

"No." She wasn't fat. He enjoyed her curviness. It made her even more luscious to hold. Skin and bones were not sexy. "I actually meant to say lazy."

He tied his other shoe, not needing to see her expression to know he'd pissed her off. Mission accomplished. Stifling a laugh, he stood and stretched, easing the aches out of his stiff muscles and warming them up before his jog.

"I'm not lazy."

"Of course not. Staying in bed instead of going for a quick and easy run with me is totally something an active person would do. This jog would probably be way too hard for you anyway." He moved into a side-lunge to stretch his legs while struggling not to smile. It was hard to tease Tessa this way, but it was also the best way to get her moving. "I'll see you when I get back."

"You're extremely irritating."

"I didn't mean to be." He'd hoped to be somewhat Tessa-style motivating too.

"For your information, I can jog around the lake."

He tried to keep the grin off his face while nodding. "I'm sure you can."

"Fine. I'll prove it. Give me two minutes to brush my teeth, pull back my hair, and find something to wear. Then I'll show you how not lazy I am."

"You don't have to prove anything to me."

She slammed the bathroom door behind her, and he let out the chuckle he'd been holding inside. He didn't know why it felt so good to get under her skin, but it did. As an added bonus, he'd have company on today's jog, something he hadn't had since leaving the city.

While he waited for her to get ready, he did a hundred pushups. Normally he did them after his run, but since he had time to kill, he wanted to stay warmed up. Halfway through a set of crunches, Tessa appeared at the bathroom door looking sexy and sporty in her black yoga capri pants, bright pink sneakers, and blue skin-tight tank. Thanks to the stretchy material he had an excellent view of her curves and couldn't wait to see them bounce around once they got outside.

"Want to warm up while I finish my set?" he asked, still sitting on the floor. The temptation to pull her to the ground on top of him was almost too overwhelming to ignore. Instead, he crunched his abs and counted to one hundred in his head. As he completed his reps, Tessa did a few halfhearted stretches while yawning, then she sat on the end of her bed, staring at him.

"Are you done yet?" she asked. "If we don't go soon, I'm changing my mind and going back to bed. I'd rather prove you wrong first."

"Let's go then," he said rising to his feet and heading out the door. Without waiting for her response, he broke into a slow and easy jog while she closed the cabin door and caught up.

"Nice. Getting a head start so I have to sprint to catch up and get tired faster. I see what you're doing. You play dirty."

"I play fair, but I'm not afraid to get dirty doing other things," he said.

"Just because we fooled around one time…" She stopped talking for a couple of breaths. "Doesn't give you permission to…talk dirty to me…"

"But seeing your cheeks turn red along with that look in your eyes that's a mix of wanting to kill me and strap me to a bed to have your way with me, is so irresistible. You make me say things I'd normally keep to myself, so my dirty talk is all your fault."

"My family could overhear you. We're hiding this from them, remember?" She panted as they crested a small slope along the trail.

"They can't hear us out here in the woods, so we can say whatever we want to each other."

The pathway narrowed and Tessa went in front of him so he could catch her if she slipped. It also meant he could watch her ass muscles moving beneath the tight workout gear. "Like for example, I could say how great your ass looks in those yoga pants and no one will overhear me."

She flapped her arms behind her as if shooing away a fly. "Stop looking at my ass. I never gave you permission to do that."

"The second you put on those leggings, you knew your ass looked fantastic. What kind of man would I be if I didn't appreciate your beautiful curves?"

"A gentleman."

"Or a dead man." He laughed.

"It's true men think about sex all the time, isn't it?" she asked.

"No, it's not. I don't think about sex all the time. At least I didn't until I laid eyes on you."

"Well, you should stop thinking about it, because it's not happening again."

"Why not? It's not like you have a real boyfriend to worry about."

"I live in the city and you live here. What's the point in fooling around when we both know it can't lead anywhere?"

"Because we both enjoyed it the first time. Because it felt fucking amazing to be inside of you. Because the thought of never touching you again makes my balls ache so fiercely I'm afraid they might actually shrivel up like raisins." He could go on and on listing all the reasons why they should have sex again, but she didn't give him the chance.

"Meh," she said simply between short puffs of breath.

"What do you mean, meh?"

Meh sounded like she was indifferent about having sex with him again. Meh sounded as if she hadn't been that thrilled by it the first time and wouldn't be the second time either. Meh sounded like a problem he'd work tirelessly to correct.

"It was good, but 'fucking amazing' is a little exaggerated, don't you think?"

He grabbed her arm, came to a halt, and spun her around to press her against a thick tree trunk. He pinned her wrists above her head with one hand, while the other snaked up under the hem of her shirt, stopping below her breast.

Tessa peered up at him with eyes full of fire and lust, and he knew in an instant she was lying about their experience together.

"I don't believe you. I see it in your eyes. You want me to taste you again…touch you." He licked her lower lip and she gasped, tilting her head toward him as if silently asking for more. Her back arched away from the tree, thrusting her breasts upward.

Accepting her invitation, his thumb brushed over the soft cup of her sports bra. It might support her while jogging, but it did little to hide the tight bud beading beneath his touch. He pinched it between his fingers. She moaned softly and her body melted, her legs spreading enough so he could put his knee between them and lean into her. She responded to the pressure with a full body vibration.

He claimed her mouth with his, taking everything she offered him. Their breaths came out in hurried pants both from the jog and from arousal. The excitement of being in the middle of nature with her in his arms was enough to make him painfully hard, even with their layers of clothing between them.

His hand left her breast and went south, slipping beneath her thin, tight pants until he found her hot, wet center. Heat radiated from her body like a furnace cranked to full blast. He dipped his fingers into her then withdrew them to rub little circles against her skin, repeating the process while she panted more heavily each time. She arched against him and thrust her tongue into his mouth, biting his lip so hard he thought he might find his release from her kisses alone.

Tessa moved her hips in time with his ministrations and within minutes that seemed to pass like seconds, she was quivering in his arms and calling out his name against his lips. She pulled away from his kiss and rested her forehead on his chest. He let go of her wrists and they fell limply to her sides for a moment before one of her hands cupped his length, stroking him.

"I want you." His voice was strained.

"I want you too," she whispered. "But we can't. Not unless you usually jog with a condom in your sock."

"My foot doesn't usually need protection." He groaned with disappointment.

"But I can…" She stroked him again, with purpose. "If you need me to…"

He wanted to say yes so badly, but there were logistics and clean up to consider.

He cupped her jaw, forcing her to look him in the eye. "As much as it kills me to jog with a hard on, I'd never ask you to do something like that here or because you feel obligated."

"But I got to… It's not exactly fair."

"Trust me. That was fun for me too." He kissed her and showed her how much he enjoyed touching her. "Let's go back before everyone else gets up and starts looking for food.

I wanted to take a shower anyway, but now I definitely need one."

He sighed when she wiggled out from between his body and the tree, already regretting his decision. "Besides, you've suddenly managed to get a nice long rest from the jog you swore would be a breeze but sounded like a marathon. I think you need to finish proving you can handle it."

The look of lust left her eyes and her stubbornness flared again. He wished his erection could switch gears that quickly.

"I bet I can beat you back to the cabin."

"Only because I gave you a much needed burst of afterglow energy."

She sprinted back the way they'd come, apparently deciding against finishing the loop.

"And only if I let you," he called after her. He wanted to sprint and catch up, but until his anatomy returned to normal, a slow and meandering jog was as fast as he could go. Today would be the last time he'd jog without a condom in his sock.

Tessa hummed as she flipped a crepe. The first batch had been filled, rolled, dusted with powdered sugared, and put into the oven to stay warm. Another few and she'd be ready to serve breakfast.

"That's a sweet sounding tune you're humming," Logan said, whispering in her ear. "I can't imagine what's put you in such a good mood."

"I don't know what you're talking about," she said, smiling and nudging him away with her elbows. "Go make your smoothies before someone sees you."

She'd been in a good mood since the jog, even though she knew she'd made a mistake with Logan again when fooling around with him was the last thing she should do. She'd wanted to stop, to say no, but hadn't. She wanted him again more than she wanted to say no. It seemed what her brain wanted and what her body wanted were two different things.

For now she couldn't focus on any of that. Getting through breakfast with her family, without them figuring out what she'd done—faking a boyfriend or sleeping with Logan—was her only priority.

"I'm finished," she said, putting the last shake of powdered sugar on the platter of rolled crepes.

"Those look deliciously fattening. Another minute to blend this up and pour it into glasses and I'll be good to go too."

He shoved a handful of spinach into the blender, which was already loaded with apple and banana. There was also some kind of little sprinkles, and slices of cucumber—although that couldn't possibly be right. No way would her family drink that concoction.

"That looks—"

He pressed the button on the blender and it whirled to life. In a matter of seconds, the jet-engine equivalent blender had turned those perfectly good apples and bananas into a jug of bright green disgustingness.

"Gross," she said, finishing her thought.

"Open minded, huh? Where'd the humming Tessa go? I like her." The way his smile lit up his eyes made her think he actually meant the words.

"She's still here, but she's not drinking that." She walked into the dining room with her platter of crepes and announced breakfast was ready. While everyone got seated around the table, she went back into the kitchen for the carafe of coffee and a pitcher of water.

The family helped themselves to the crepes, added whipped cream and syrup while Logan passed out glasses of his "famous" green smoothie. Possibly the only thing it would be famous for at this family gathering would be as the only beverage not consumed by anyone.

"How are the crepes?" she asked, taking a few for her plate and passing the platter to Logan.

Murmurs of thanks and appreciation went around the table. Mouths were too full for polite conversation.

Logan looked around the table eyeing the untouched smoothies. "So this is my 'famous' green smoothie. I can tell you're all eager to try it. I won't bore you with the details of everything that's in it, but it's very healthy and delicious, and will give you more energy than that third cup of coffee."

"Sounds great," Mary said, not reaching for her glass.

"I'll try it after I finish the crepes. I don't want to tarnish my taste buds," Sally said.

"I'll stick to coffee, thanks," Joe said. "But I'm sure it's great for the younger generation. You guys are always into weird things."

The enthusiasm on Logan's face vanished, replaced by disappointment and something resembling hurt. Tessa's chest constricted. She'd known none of them would like it, but she'd thought they'd at least try it to be polite. As much as she wanted to win, she didn't want Logan hurt by her family's rejection.

Willing her gag reflex to stay calm, she grabbed her glass. "I had no idea you guys were such chickens. It's just a green smoothie. How bad can it be?" She suppressed a shiver at the thought of her last green juice experience in the city. She'd barely gotten through half the bottle before gagging. Three bucks down the drain. Literally. And she still couldn't smell cucumber without a wave of nausea hitting her. But this wasn't juice, it was a smoothie and there were a bunch of other non-green and delicious ingredients in it. She'd seen them in there original form, even if she couldn't see them now.

It's just apples and bananas. Apples and bananas…

The first sensation was thickness. Not at all like the thin juice she'd had before. This was more milkshake consistency. Then came the sweet apple and the creaminess of the banana.

She swallowed. "Delicious," she said half-truthfully. "You should try it. It's not nearly as bad as it looks."

"Thanks. I think." Logan looked perkier again.

"What were the sprinkle looking things you put in there?" she asked, still curious about that ingredient.

"Chia seeds. They change consistence when you put them into liquid. They're super healthy."

She took another sip, almost looking forward to the fresh, fruity taste, until something slimy and round hit the back of her tongue. Must be the chia. She held the liquid in her mouth, afraid to swallow for fear her gag reflex would trigger. The longer it sat in her mouth, the more the sensation intensified. Cutting off a large chunk of crepe, she quickly swallowed the smoothie, then shoveled in the crepe, chewed and swallowed again.

Logan could literally cry, but she would never put another mouthful of that green demon concoction into her mouth. Nope. She glanced around the table. Only Mary had reached for her glass. Sweet and kindhearted Mary. She was in for a rude awakening, because Tessa had lied. The drink was awful.

"Looks gross, no offense, Logan," Mary said after taking a few quick sips, "but actually tastes good."

Mary was being generous. It was passable as a food product, but not something she'd look forward to consuming again. Ever. For all eternity. It could be the only cure to something that was about to kill her and she'd still think twice about drinking it.

Logan gave up encouraging anyone else to drink the smoothies.

"So what are everyone's plans for the day?" Martha asked.

A mixture of relaxing in the sun, fishing on the dock, and playing cards sounded from around the table. Tessa had no idea what she would do, but after her early morning jog and making breakfast, she was ready for a nap. Logan was the only one who didn't speak up with his plans for the day.

"What about you? Any big plans?" she asked him.

He shrugged. "I thought I might do a little yoga before I perfect my paddle boarding skills."

"I've always wanted to try yoga, but there's nowhere to do that in town and those videos always seem so cheesy," Sally said.

"You're welcome to join me if you want. Everyone is."

"Is it hard?" Mary asked.

"When you become more advanced the movements do get more difficult, but I wasn't planning on doing anything tricky. I think you'd all be fine."

"Except for Tessa. Remember the tree pose the other night?"

"It was dark and the twinkling campfire threw off my depth perception," she said.

"Sure. It's the campfire's fault," James said teasingly.

Tessa laughed along with them, a sense of warmth washing over her instead of the usual defensiveness. "I'm warning you, that campfire is evil with its smoke and marshmallow-roasting coals."

They all laughed again until James suddenly stopped, a serious expression on his face. "Did Tessa make a joke when we were teasing her?"

Everyone got quiet and peered at Tessa.

"Did something happen on the mountain yesterday?" Mary asked.

Tessa felt her cheeks burn hot at the memory of Logan and her naked at the lookout. She glanced in his direction and if she wasn't mistaken, his expression was one of both achievement and guilt.

"I don't…" She started to defend herself but didn't know what to say. She was usually a good liar, but not when her pink cheeks were about to give her away.

"I think I know the truth," Sally said.

Tessa bit her lip and reached under the table to squeeze Logan's leg, indicating he needed to think of something believable, fast.

"She got abducted by aliens. That has to be it."

She sighed when they laughed.

"Well, whatever's gotten into you lately, it's doing you good. I haven't seen you glow like this in ages." Martha smiled contentedly.

Logan put his hand on hers and when she met his gaze, he winked, as if acknowledging that he was the thing that had gotten into her lately and had done her good. She couldn't deny it.

He had, and he had been good. And the afterglow of sex with Logan apparently lasted days.

Chapter Fifteen

Logan didn't have yoga mats with him, so he'd spread out towels instead. The sandy beach near their dock would be soft enough for them to be on their knees or backs while they worked through a series of beginner yoga movements.

Mary, Sally, and Martha were already there when Tessa walked up. "Room for one more?"

"Of course," he said and laid out another towel.

"You're actually doing yoga? This I gotta see," Travis said, turning his lawn chair around on the dock so he could still fish but also have a better view of the yoga session.

"I'll have you know I already went for a long jog this morning and am still going to do yoga while you sit on your butt fishing." She raised her chin defiantly.

"You jogged? Wow. Logan, you must've made a convincing argument. Did you tell her spiders were chasing her?" He laughed and cast his line into the water.

"Nope. I implied she couldn't keep up with me. Worked like a charm." He grinned, thinking back to their morning exercise, not all of it jogging.

"Nice trick." Sally patted him on the shoulder. Her eyes bulged when her hand landed on his muscular body. She turned toward Tessa and mouthed "wow" before taking her hand back and finding her place. Tessa grinned and nodded.

The sisters were anything but subtle, not that he minded their approval. Forcing his mind away from Tessa's body writhing beneath his touch, he focused on getting them in the proper accomplished seated pose to get started. He cleared his mind and guided them to breathe in through their noses and out through their mouths. Once he felt centered, he did a few simple poses, pausing in downward dog for a few minutes, getting the full stretch.

He assessed their movements with each pose, making verbal suggestions for slight corrections as he saw needed and once or twice having to physically adjust their arms or legs to get the positions right and prevent injury. Tessa had been doing well, until now. With her feet together and her legs way too far out behind her, she looked as if she were doing some kind of pushup instead of downward dog.

"Can I get you into the right position?" he asked. The word position in reference to Tessa made him ache for what he hadn't been able to finish with her on the trail this morning.

"Am I doing it wrong?"

"A little bit. Move your feet apart and walk your hands back while lifting your hips toward the sky. Like this."

He slipped around behind her and put his hands on her hips, gently guiding her up and back toward him until she was bent over in front of him in a position that made him wish they were alone. Running his hand down the back of her thighs, he noted her tight hamstrings. "Feel that pulling right there? That will help your muscles loosen up. Our jog made this whole area stiff."

"Should we leave you two alone?" Mary asked.

"You guys need a room?" Sally asked.

"They didn't need one yesterday," Travis said with a big grin on his face.

Tessa's head shot up and she glared over her shoulder at him. Before he could tell her how to get out of the pose safely, she dropped to her stomach with a grunt. Logan was left hovering over her and praying they didn't notice any tenting in the vicinity of his groin.

"I was helping her with her position," he said, feeling guilty and defensive.

"What's this about yesterday?" Sally asked, standing and looking eager for gossip.

"They went skinny dipping," Travis explained with the aid of air quotes. "But we all know what that leads to."

"You told him?" Tessa stood, folding her arms across her chest.

"About the skinny dipping, yes. About how it was hot after we hiked up the mountain and we shared the same water source to cool off. That's it," he said, stressing the last point quietly so hopefully only she would hear.

"But there's more, isn't there?" Mary asked, grinning. "You two did it up there, didn't you?"

"Mary! Mom is standing right beside you!" Tessa shrieked, looking as guilty as he felt.

"But you did, didn't you?" Sally and Mary high-fived. "Told you it'd work."

What was that?

Tessa must've heard the same comment because her guilty expression quickly faded into one of suspicion. "Did you high-five your sister having sex?"

"She admits it! I knew it. You didn't come right out and say it, but I knew it as soon as you mentioned the skinny dipping," Travis said.

Logan didn't know if he should feel embarrassed or proud, but he did know he did not feel the least bit relaxed like he usually did after a yoga session.

Tessa visibly shook beside him. "You told her what would work?" she asked through clenched teeth.

"Tessa-bear, it's no big deal." Martha stepped toward her daughter, but Tessa put her hands up to as if to keep her away.

"What's no big deal, Mom?"

"We knew you'd hit it off with Logan if given the chance, that's all."

Tessa sucked in a breath. They'd been set up. This week, he'd thought he'd been invited out as a kind gesture because he was new to town and Travis's friend, but they'd wanted to fix him up with Tessa, and it had worked. He couldn't be angry with them. They're matchmaking tactics might not be the most upfront, but they were effective.

"This was all a big matchmaking scheme? I should've known," she whispered. Her stunned gaze focused on Mary. "You didn't have to go into town with James yesterday, did you? You bailed on the hike to force me and Logan together."

"I didn't hear you complaining when you got back last night."

"You both seemed happy with your hike."

"I'm not surprised you fooled Logan and me both into coming here this week. I mean, it's not the first time you've tried to set me up with someone." She shook her head. "But even after you knew I had a boyfriend in the city, you still went through with it. Why would you keep trying to fix us up when you know I'm dating someone already?"

"We thought it wouldn't hurt to see if there was any chemistry between you and Logan and apparently there is," Martha said, looking away. "You never even mentioned that guy in the city before so, I guess, we just didn't think he meant very much to you."

"Besides, you can't be serious about your boyfriend if you're doing Logan," Sally blurted.

Tessa's mouth dropped open, then she turned on her heel

and left him to face her family alone. What could he say? What her family did was wrong, at least as far as Tessa was concerned, but yet, a part of him wanted to thank them. Tessa was everything he wanted in a woman and somehow they thought he was a good match for her.

"I think we'll have to finish this yoga class another time. I better go talk to her. I'll see you guys later." He left the towels on the ground.

They could clean up his yoga mess while he cleaned up their matchmaking mess.

Tessa didn't look up from her sketchbook when the door to the cabin opened. Logan strode into the room and sat on the end of her bed instead of his own. He grabbed her foot in his strong hand and rubbed his thumbs along her arch.

"What are you doing?" she asked, not pulling her foot away.

"Rubbing your foot. You seem like you could use a massage."

"Thanks. That feels good." Surprisingly good, but she still couldn't relax.

"Are you okay?" he asked.

"I've been better."

"Want to talk about it?"

"What's there to talk about? My family went behind my back again." She shrugged. It was all so tiresome. Why couldn't they let her make her own decisions in life?

She put down her sketchbook unable to concentrate when she was annoyed. He seemed unconcerned about everything. "You didn't know, did you?" *If he did…*

What would she do, take back sleeping with him?

"Of course not."

"Then why don't you care that they meddled in your life

too? Or that they only invited you here to fix you up with me?" she asked, sitting forward so they were only inches apart.

He shrugged. "Because their plan worked out pretty great."

"It's all about the sex for you then, huh?"

"That's not what I said." He sighed. "They thought we'd get along and, guess what? We do."

"It's not terrible for you. You want to be here. You want to settle down in Cutter's Creek. I don't want another reason to be pressured into moving home. This isn't the first time they've meddled in my life." She pulled her foot back and bent her knees, wrapping her arms around her legs protectively. "Not to mention that as far as they're concerned, I've now cheated on my boyfriend. They're so frustrating!"

"No one thinks you're a bad person for what we did."

She sprang up from the bed, irritated completely. "But that's who they made me become by playing their little matchmaking game. Even though they knew I had a boyfriend, they still set me up with you. I still slept with you."

"And did they seem like they were upset about it?"

"No!"

"So relax."

"Relax? That's your big helpful suggestion?"

"You could tell them the truth that there is no Dick in the city." He smirked.

"You love saying that, don't you?"

He half shrugged. "Sort of. You picked a crappy name for a fake boyfriend. You should have gone with something better like…Marco."

"Why is Marco better than Richard?"

"Because Richard easily becomes Dick, but Marco, well, he stays Marco and sounds all exotic. Marco." He wiggled his eyebrows as he said the name in a low, sexy voice.

She couldn't stop the giggle that bubbled up from her

chest. "I think you want to date Marco." She tried to copy his tone and sexiness, but it came out sounding ridiculous.

"I don't swing that way. I'm all about the Tessa in my life." He pulled her up against the side of the bed. "But next week you'll be back in the city finding another Dick to date for real and I'll be here, alone. So…" He shrugged. "I guess I'll have to find someone else too."

Her chest constricted at the thought of him with another woman, a woman she would no doubt know from town. Another woman she'd known for years would soon put her hands on his body, touch him, move with him… The image made her queasy. But why should she care? He was right. In a couple of days, she'd be back in the city, like she wanted, and hopefully she would meet a man to date.

"You're okay with that? With us…like this…like that in a week?"

"Do I have any other choice? You're leaving. I'm staying. End of story, like you said."

She bit the inside of her cheek knowing she should stay silent but unable to resist asking the question on her mind. "You're not going to say I should stay?" Did she want him too? Wouldn't that be as bad as her family doing the same thing?

"No." He pulled her down onto the bed and lounged next to her, propped up on one elbow. "You hate when your family asks you to stay. I'm not about to give you another reason to hate me when you only started tolerating me."

She stroked her hands along his back. "You are pretty insufferable sometimes."

"Like when I do this?" he asked, then kissed her neck and pulled her shirt to the side to kiss her collarbone. His hand traveled down her side and wrapped around her hip to squeeze her rear. "Or this?"

"Totally, but remember, we weren't supposed to do this again." Even as she said the words, she knew she didn't mean them.

"Is that why you bought condoms at the store?" he asked. He slid his hand up to cup her breast. When he touched her, every part of her begged for more.

"How do you know that?"

"We share a bathroom. I saw them in your bag of odd supplies."

How could she explain the hodgepodge of things she'd randomly thrown in her basket but didn't actually need? "I'm not constipated," she blurted.

He laughed.

"I grabbed that by accident."

"Embarrassed to buy condoms?" he asked.

"No. I needed other things. Those were…an impulse buy." An impulse buy that took her three tries to work up the nerve to grab. He didn't need to know that tidbit.

"Whatever you gotta tell yourself, but I know the truth. You want me. I'd hate to see that box of condoms you bought go to waste."

He kissed her and her body instantly responded. A pressure built low in her belly and he was the only one who could ease it.

Regardless of where she was next week, she wanted Logan right here, right now.

Sliding her hand down his back and under the waistband of his shorts, she cupped his gloriously sculpted ass. Every part of his body was a muscular treat.

"I have to say, when I first met you I thought you were more likely to bench press tree trunks than do complicated yoga poses. But seeing you on your mat today…" She squeezed his ass, thinking about how good it had looked in his gym shorts. "You looked pretty fantastic."

"So did you." He quickly stood from the bed and pulled her to her feet in front of him. Tugging her tank top over her head, he tossed it to the ground then added her bra to the pile. "You looked amazing doing those poses. Each one made me want to do them with you. Naked."

He sucked her nipple into his mouth, teasing it stiff with his tongue and teeth. She arched into him, wanting more. She threaded her fingers into his short, cropped hair, holding his head in place while he sent bolts of electricity through her breasts to her belly.

When he pulled back, she pressed her mouth to his. Her kiss was anything but gentle and loving. It was raw and needy. It was every emotion she'd been fighting to stay away from him rolled into one hot, wet kiss. They breathed each other in, tongues twining, teeth biting.

Her breasts heaved as she gulped in huge breaths while she tugged his shirt over his head. Dropping to her knees, she took his shorts with her, pooling them on the floor around his ankles.

Without hesitation, she took him into her mouth. He was hard and ready for her, thrusting his hips slightly in time with her movements. She used her hands and mouth to glide along his length, each stroke eliciting a moan of pleasure from deep in his chest.

Logan fisted his hand in her hair slowing her pace as if he wanted to stretch every second into minutes.

"Stop, Tessa. You're too much." Her pulled her to standing and kissed her hard on the mouth. "I think we need your box of condoms now."

"The whole box?" she asked, feeling lightheaded and drunk with lust.

"Only if you ask nicely."

She grabbed the box from the bathroom and was still struggling to open it when she rejoined his side. With one hand holding the box and the other hand trying unsuccessfully to tear it open, she was too preoccupied to stop Logan when he unceremoniously stripped her of her capri pants and panties.

"Give me that," he said, taking the box and ripping it open in one quick motion. In another second he had a foil packet opened and tossed to the floor. As she watched him roll the condom onto his erection, she bit her lip, anticipation building.

When his hands were free, he spun her around and held her back against his chest for a moment, kissing her shoulder. He caressed her breasts and whispered in her ear. "I couldn't stop imagining this earlier. Seeing you in downward dog…"

He bent her forward until her hands held her up on the bed, then ran his hands along her spine as he stood behind her. Tapping the inside of her ankle with his toes, she spread her feet apart knowing that's what he wanted.

He groaned and touched the backs of her thighs like he had earlier, adjusting her position, then eased into her heat. Tessa closed her eyes and let her head drop, enjoying the feeling of Logan moving inside of her. She'd promised herself she wouldn't do this with him again. But damn. He was worth the heartache later.

He pulled out slowly then drove into her fast, hitting hard and deep. She called out her pleasure as he repeated the motion over and over. When his hand slipped around her waist and found her hot center, rubbing circles on her sensitive skin, she lost control. Her body trembled with his touch. As he sped up his pace, she moved against him until she couldn't hold back anymore. Calling out his name, she tumbled over the edge of euphoria into oblivion. A moment later, he followed her.

As they lay on her bed in each other's arms, she couldn't stop her thoughts from going back to her family's plan and deviousness. She was still mad that they'd interfered with her life, but their actions had led to her current post-orgasm contentedness. A tiny part of her was happy they'd fixed her up with Logan. But she'd never admit that out loud.

Chapter Sixteen

Tessa sat cross-legged in front of the roaring fireplace, enjoying the dancing flames and the heat radiating from the hearth. They'd planned on a bonfire tonight, but Mother Nature had other plans and shortly after dinner, the sky opened up above them. Rain hadn't stopped pouring down since.

She didn't mind so much. Less chance of spiders inside meant she had an easier time relaxing. Or she would've been more relaxed if she hadn't found out about the matchmaking scheme earlier. The sting of her family's betrayal still hadn't worn off fully.

Currently, they were playing a round of poker. She didn't have it in her to join the fun, because it didn't feel fun right now. It felt like she was an outsider looking in, the same way she'd always felt. Here she had this amazing family, as Logan had pointed out, and yet she never felt like she could enjoy her time with them because she didn't fit in. She was the one who didn't want to live and die in town, the one who wanted to paint and travel. The one who looked at the lake and saw colors and textures, not fish.

A cheer went up from around the table as Logan won another hand. Part of her wanted to go sit by his side and cheer him on, but doing so would only prove to her family that they'd been right in setting them up. The last thing they needed was encouragement. Even though her family pissed her off with their newest trick, she couldn't deny that she missed them so much it physically hurt.

In the city, she'd been so busy painting and pitching her art to galleries that she didn't have time to think about everyone back home. But being here she'd instantly felt the connections she'd been missing. Her family was awesome in every way, except when they were meddling in her life.

Maybe she'd been too hard on them this week. Maybe she'd gotten overly upset because she knew they were right. Logan was a good match. He was amazing. If she'd met him in the city, she'd be head over heels for him.

"Tessa, would you mind grabbing me a water? I hate to get up from the table in case I break my winning streak against Travis." Logan peered over his shoulder, giving her the look that told her he'd asked for water, but was currently picturing her delivering it naked. The thought made her need a glass of cold water too—dumped over her head to cool her off so she could think straight.

"Sure," she said, rising from the floor. She quickly grabbed his drink from the kitchen then wandered over to his side at the table.

He pushed his chair back and pulled her down onto his lap, wrapping his free hand securely around her waist. "Thanks, sugar."

"Logan, don't," she whispered. She wasn't into showing public displays of affection as it was but certainly wasn't into it with the guy she was supposedly cheating on her boyfriend with.

"What? They already know about us."

She tried to wiggle away, but he held her tight and whispered in her ear so only she would hear. "Keep wiggling on my lap and I won't be able to stand from this table without giving your family an eyeful I'd rather be for your eyes only."

Heat flashed through her and she stilled. His hand settled on her upper thigh, below the level of the table where her family would see. It was enough that they'd see her sitting on his lap, they didn't need to see him touching her body too.

For as obvious as Logan's affection was, her family did a remarkable job of ignoring it, almost as if they knew that by drawing attention to it, it would end. Or maybe they were too busy basking in their success to point out the obvious. Together, Tessa and Logan played a few hands, with her input into what cards to keep. Every time, they'd lost. After the fourth failure in a row, she twisted on Logan's lap to face him.

"I think I should go back to the fireplace. You were winning before I joined you. I'm apparently bad luck."

"You're not bad luck," James said, sounding surprisingly supportive. "For me. Stay. Cuddle with Logan."

"I'm not cuddling," she said shifting to stand.

Logan held her still. "Stay. I'm sure our luck will change."

Will it? Would anything change for them in the near future?

"I'll pull up a chair and sit beside you instead, okay?"

He nodded and she moved a chair from the other side of the table as the game continued. Logan did better without her input, not that she noticed. While he collected his winnings, she picked up her phone. She'd gotten a bad signal all day, but finally she was showing three bars instead of one. Clicking over to her email, she checked her inbox. The program searched for a few seconds then loaded four new messages—two newsletters for clothing she couldn't afford, a cell phone bill, and one from the last gallery she'd been waiting on. Her heart pounded in her ears. Fingers trembling with hope and anticipation, she clicked open.

Thank you for your inquiry about placing your art with our gallery, however…

Her eyes blurred and she couldn't see the rest of the words. She didn't need to—another rejection. This one stung worse than the others. It had been her top choice and the one she'd waited the longest to hear back from. The one she'd pinned all her hopes on to come through in the end.

"Are you okay?" Logan asked, putting his hand on her shoulder. "What's happened?"

"It's nothing. I don't want to talk about it." Couldn't talk about it. The pain of rejection stabbed her in the gut and she feared if she began talking about it, there'd be no stopping all the things she'd been trapping inside from spilling out.

"If that finance guy of yours in the city has said something to make our Tessa-bear this upset, I might take a trip into the city to kick some ass," her dad said, sitting forward with a concerned look on his face. He was always a mild-mannered man until someone messed with his family.

"Dad, please. Be serious."

"I am serious."

Her brother and Travis agreed.

"Don't let some guy treat you like crap," Sally said.

"You're too good to let someone make you this upset," Mary added.

Martha nodded. "You tell that boyfriend of yours you don't need him anymore. You've got Logan now."

"It's not that." Did they think she was so weak and pathetic that she couldn't live without a man by her side? A man was a choice in her life, not a necessity. Well, Richard had been a bit of a necessity since his whole purpose was to protect her from her family's nagging and meddling, which hadn't worked out quite as planned.

"You tell him to take a hike then we'll go get your stuff." Her mom continued talking with everyone else as if Tessa wasn't even there. "We'll have her settled back into her old room by Monday."

"I'm not moving back," she said. The talking continued around her. "Would you listen to me? I'm not moving home. I didn't get dumped." Her voice rose with her annoyance level.

"Tessa, don't get upset. They're worried about you," Logan said. She was pretty sure he was trying to comfort and support her, but all he did was support her family instead of the woman he claimed to care about.

"It wasn't from Richard. There is no Richard," she said, louder than before. They stopped to stare at her. "It was from a gallery I hoped would want my art, but like every other gallery, they said no. Happy now?"

Faces gawked at her from around the table and it felt like a full minute before anyone spoke.

"There's no Richard?"

"Is that what she said?"

"That's what I heard."

They all spoke at once, and none of them even seemed to have heard the part about her broken dreams. Irritation built inside her, each comment strengthening her anger.

"Did you make him up?" Sally asked.

"Why would you do something like that to us?" Mary asked, having the nerve to sound hurt.

"Why did you lie to us?" her mother asked, her voice trembling.

Something inside Tessa snapped. "Did any of you even hear me say the last gallery I applied to rejected me? Do you only care I made up some stupid boyfriend?"

"Why did you lie to us about Richard?"

"Because I didn't want you guys to fix me up with anyone or nag me to move home. Seemed my plan failed on both accounts because there's no stopping you. So here's the truth. My glamorous art career consists of painting murals on shop windows because no one will hang my art in their gallery. And I don't have a boyfriend. I haven't had time to meet anyone because I've been too busy trying to earn enough money to pay rent. Satisfied?"

Tessa rose from her chair and walked out the door leaving them behind in a stunned silence. The truth was out and tomorrow they'd hound her even more to move home, but at least she didn't have anything to hide anymore. Of course, that also meant she couldn't hide from the truth either. Speaking it out loud had somehow made it more real.

Her life in the city wasn't all she'd dreamed it would be, but living in Cutter's Creek wasn't what she wanted either. So where did that leave her?

L ogan looked around the cabin surprised to find it empty. He needed to find Tessa, talk to her, make sure she was okay. Her family meant well, he knew that, but they came off all wrong.

He walked back outside, peering into the darkness for any hint of where she could be. All vehicles were accounted for. She would never brave a walk along a trail in the dark. Not only was she smarter than that, but she'd be too afraid of seeing spiders lurking nearby to risk it.

Near the water's edge, a pinpoint of light beckoned him like a lighthouse.

A sliver of moon hung in the clear, star-filled sky now that the rain had stopped and the clouds had blown away. Even from here he could see the reflections off the calm surface of the lake and knew the light he saw was Tessa, probably with her sketchbook open and working.

He rifled through his bag for a minute until he found the small box he needed, then wandered toward her. Taking a seat on the dock next to her, he stared out at the lake, unspeaking. She was sketching, and from what he could see it was another amazing scene. He hated to interrupt her while she worked, but he also couldn't allow her to be unhappy and alone.

He placed the small box on her knee. "I got you a little something in town."

She glanced down to the gift and reached for it, hesitating for a second before opening it. She rubbed her thumbs over the little colored sticks through the window in the packaging. "These are great. But why the gift?"

He shrugged. "When I first saw your sketches they reminded me of this picture I saw once. The artist had drawn scenic landscapes like you and used pastels. I thought you could try them. Might be a fun change from your usual pencil work."

"This was nice of you," she said, meeting his gaze. Even in the low light, he could read the range of emotion in her eyes tonight. "Thank you, Logan. This is so sweet of you."

"You're welcome."

When he peered into her eyes, he felt as if he could see her soul, as if the wall she kept up around everyone else was suddenly invisible and she let him in fully to know the real Tessa, not the girl she wanted people to see, but the woman she was on the inside. When she looked at him with this expression, he would hike up Kilimanjaro if she asked. He'd do anything to make her feel better, to take away her pain, and to make her keep looking at him like this, with this look of…love in her eyes. Or maybe that was how he looked at her.

"If it's any consolation, they were all sorry to hear about the gallery," he said, leaning forward to rest his elbows on his knees. "I think they were in shock to learn about your fake boyfriend."

She didn't speak, just sketched.

"I'm sorry the gallery said no. Was it one you wanted?"

Sniffling, she wiped her nose with a tissue and nodded. "Yeah. I should've known there was no way they'd want me. I'm out of my league. I mean, who am I anyway? Nobody."

"That's not true. Your work is great. It's the city that sucks." His chest ached for her. If only there was something he could do to take her pain away, to ease her self-doubt, restore her faith in herself. Maybe he could help, in some small way, because at least he understood life in the city better than her family could. He'd lived and worked there. He'd been chewed up and spit out too. He'd had his dreams squashed like a cockroach. If anyone understood her right now, it was him.

"I know how it feels to pin all your hopes and dreams on the opportunity you see in the city only to have them fall short and leave you crushed."

"Yeah? How?" Her hand continued to move over the page, filling in little details. Every stroke of her pencil brought the picture to life more and more. Even if he hadn't been seeing the moment firsthand, her picture would've completely captured the mood and tone of the scene before him.

"This gym teacher job in Cutter's Creek isn't my first time in the classroom. I was a teacher in the city for a few years too. I loved working with the kids and seeing them get better at sports and have a healthy attitude, but at the end of the day, I still felt dissatisfied with life. I didn't like having to follow a set of guidelines that weren't my own. Showing up at school early, staying late, filling out report cards, none of it was my thing. The only stuff I enjoyed was when a parent would come to me to ask advice about how to help their kid be healthier or improve at a sport they loved. I felt energized to make a plan for them."

He paused to clear his head. Thinking back about his time in the city, it was still hard to deal with the overwhelming disappointment. For a place he'd called home his whole life, he felt little love for it.

"I'm not sure I see the connection. Seems like you had a good thing." She put her book on the dock beside them and followed his gaze out to the lake.

"I finally realized the stuff that made me the happiest was the stuff I only got to do once in a while. So I made the choice to quit teaching and become a personal trainer instead. I figured if what I loved was creating a health plan for students, then I should do that full-time. Sort of like how you know you love art and want to do it full-time."

"Is that when you opened your gym?"

He sighed. How many times had he asked himself if there was something different he could've done to keep the gym running? "I used my entire savings to open my gym in this space around the corner from my place. I figured it was a good location—near lots of residential housing and there wasn't a huge brand name gym within a few blocks, and the rent was almost affordable. So I went for it. But I could never figure out how to get a steady stream of people through the doors. I'd get a few, but not enough to bring in the rent check each month. I tried advertising and different hours. I added more services and tried to create an option for everyone, but it didn't work. I couldn't compete with the bigger gyms. Even though they were farther away, it didn't matter. Eventually, I was out of money, out of options, and out of energy."

"I'm sorry. It sucks to see your dream not work out like that."

"Yes, it does. The city is a rough place for people like us. People who have big dreams but few resources at our disposal. New York can be the place that makes those dreams come to fruition, or it can be the place that ruins you."

"If you could do it all again, would you?" she asked.

"In a heartbeat. Only this time I'll do things differently.

At least, it's what I'm hoping to do in Cutter's Creek."

"But why here? Doesn't seem like the best place for opportunity."

"It's the perfect place. It's too small for any big name gyms to set up shop here. The closest one is more than an hour away. Here the people are loyal. I think if I open a gym with fair prices that everyone can afford with services catering to each type of person, I can make it work."

"What about the gym itself? Would it be set up the same way inside? What would it look like?" Her tone was filled with enthusiasm. Even in her time of disappointment, she could still be happy and excited for him. His heart swelled.

As he rattled off where he would put the equipment so the space would be used most efficiently, she picked up her sketchbook, flipped to a new page, and opened the box of oil pastels. He lounged back and folded his hands under his head as he looked up to the stars. In his mind's eye, he could already picture the gym in such detail it made him long for the day he'd see it in real life. There was no doubt that it would exist eventually, only a matter of when.

He stopped talking and cleared his throat, suddenly aware of how long he'd been going on about his future gym. All along, Tessa had quietly murmured acknowledgements. "Sorry, I shouldn't have bored you with all that detail."

"No. I like hearing about your gym. It sounds like it'll be a great place."

He sat up and nuzzled her shoulder. "What have you been working on?"

"This," she said, not hiding her work this time, but instead holding up her book so he could get a good look.

If he could take a snapshot of the dream gym he saw in his head, this sketch would be almost identical. How she'd gotten so many of the details right by only listening to his descriptions was like magic.

"This is incredible. I can't believe you did this while I talked."

"Does it look a little like you imagined?"

"Are you kidding? It looks exactly like I imagined." He cupped her jaw in his hands and kissed her lips. She kissed him back more eagerly than he expected, her tongue slipping into his mouth, finding his and dancing with it. If he could have her on the dock without fear of her family finding them, he would in a second. He wanted to feel her body next to his, cuddle her, comfort her, thank her for her amazing talent, and for listening to him talk about his passion. He hadn't realized how deeply he cared for her and how much her opinion meant to him. Hearing her support for his career and his hopes for the future pushed him over the edge, and he couldn't imagine spilling his guts to anyone else, ever.

"You like it?" she asked.

"I love…" He stumbled over the word suddenly wanting to say something he wasn't sure he was ready for, something he suddenly felt so completely that it shocked him. Instead of dealing with it, he forced it from his mind. "I love it. The sketch. It's perfect."

She smiled then kissed his cheek. A gentle, simple kiss that left his chest feeling full, as if his heart might suddenly burst through his ribs. He pulled back and ignored the sensation, moving the topic back to something safe, like her struggle in the city. "I can't believe galleries could look at work like this and decide not to show your stuff."

"I would never show a gallery this stuff." She shook her head and chuckled. "I've been painting cityscapes and showing those to the galleries. They're turning out great so I don't know what's wrong with them."

"Since I've never seen one, I couldn't comment on whether they're great or awful, but I can tell you these sketches are unbelievable. If the galleries aren't interested in the paintings, then it couldn't hurt to show them a few of these."

She laughed like he'd told the funniest joke she'd heard in a long time. "No way. I could never show them this stuff. Who wants to hang stupid landscapes from Cutter's Creek on their wall?"

I would.

"Show them whatever you're comfortable with, but maybe it's time to mix things up, give them something that's still you, but with a twist. A new angle. Who knows, maybe it'll be the thing they've been looking for."

She mumbled a response and nodded, but didn't look convinced.

He wished there was a way where she could live her dream of having her art hang in a big gallery while also getting to be with her. But short of moving back to the city, he didn't see that happening. And moving back would mean giving up the chance to follow his dreams.

No matter how much he was falling for Tessa, their hopes for the future were taking them in two different directions. Someone would have to sacrifice everything for the other. He couldn't ask Tessa to do that anymore than he could do it himself. How was it that he'd come to Cutter's Creek for a fresh chance to get the future he dreamed of, only to fall for a girl who wanted the life he'd left back in the city?

Chapter Seventeen

"Thanks for driving me into town," Tessa said, as Logan pulled his car into James's auto shop. "It shouldn't take me too long to fill out the paperwork and pick up my rental. We could always meet up for lunch after."

"Sounds good. I have an appointment to check out a possible gym space but that should only take twenty minutes. What's your favorite lunch place?" he asked.

They didn't have a ton of restaurant options, but she'd always loved Randy's Diner. She'd been going there her whole life and the food hadn't changed, ever. Randy didn't like change, and in this one circumstance she was grateful for that.

"Have you been to the diner yet?"

"No. Should we go there?" he asked.

"I'll meet you outside and we'll go in together so I can introduce you to Randy, okay?" She couldn't wait to see the look on his face when they walked in. It wasn't a typical diner with chrome and vinyl and Formica. It was rustic country, and every square inch of the place paid homage to Randy's obsession with old western movies and books.

She climbed out of the car and after feeling the heat of the sun for a millisecond she slipped off her light sweater. "Mind if I leave this in here? I'm already super hot." As she leaned back into the car, his gaze dipped to her cleavage.

"I agree," he said, clearly not talking about the sunny day.

"Men," she muttered as she put her sweater down on the car seat on top of her sketchbook. She'd brought it with the thought that she might stop somewhere to draw but between getting her rental back and having lunch, there was no reason to lug her art supplies around with her. She could trust Logan with them until she had time to use them later.

Logan shrugged. "I can't help but appreciate the view."

Knowing his eyes were on her body made her want to climb back in the car and find another lookout spot to fool around in. Or maybe she wanted to get him alone so she could have him to herself some more. If she were honest, that was why she'd asked him out for a lunch date. Although, it wasn't a date, simply two people eating together. But she knew when they got back to the campground they'd be expected to hang out with her family. At the beginning of the week she would have done anything to keep her distance from Logan, but in the last couple of days, something changed.

She loved how interested he was in her art and her life. She loved his passion for his fitness career and his desire to be his own boss again. Most importantly, she loved the way they seemed to connect on so many levels. Not only sexually, but emotionally and mentally too.

The thought that their time together would be over in a couple of days when everyone went back to their regular lives sat in her stomach like a lump of bad seafood. She felt sick thinking about what it would be like not having him around to hang out with and talk to. Or kiss.

"I'll see you later." She stood again and watched him pull

out of the parking lot. What would happen when she didn't see him anymore? Her heart fluttered.

She'd known going into this that hooking up with Logan was a limited-time offer. She knew they'd never have any kind of future together when she planned to go back to the city and he stayed here. And she'd known getting involved with him could make things more complicated than she wanted to deal with. However, once she'd gotten to know Logan, it had become impossible to stay away from him.

Now she was screwed. Her heart wanted to keep him close, but her mind knew she had to leave him to pursue her dreams. She couldn't have both.

She pulled open the shop door and scanned the service area for her brother so she could collect the keys. In two days, she was driving back to the city and leaving Cutter's Creek behind again. Exactly what she wanted, right? But if this was what she wanted, why did the thought of heading down that highway, alone, make her eyes sting with newly formed tears?

Logan shook hands with the realtor. "That has most of what I'm looking for, but I might want to think about it a little. Is there a big rush to make an offer?"

"Not that I know of, but you never can tell who will see a property and decide it's right for them. If anything else comes available, I'll let you know. Right now, I think this suits your needs pretty well."

"What about that place around the corner, the one with the lakefront view? The principal at the school mentioned it was coming on the market."

Vince sighed. "It might be, but the owner was hoping it would become something like a museum, not a gym filled with meatheads whose muscles were bigger than their brains.

Her words, not mine."

Logan groaned. He was sick of the stereotype that because he cared about his physical strength he didn't have room left in his brain for other intelligent thoughts. "Tell her I'm not a meathead. I was a business owner in New York City. I'm not an idiot."

"She's reluctant to sell to an outsider. The older generation in town have some hesitation when it comes to new people."

"Just the older people, huh? Is that why it took me hounding your office every day last week to get a chance to see this place?"

Vince shrugged again, looking embarrassed. "I've got to run to another appointment. Think about this place and we'll be in touch soon."

Vince left Logan standing on the sidewalk, annoyed and confused. Why did the people of Cutter's Creek dislike outsiders so much? It wasn't like he was a serial killer. He wanted to open a gym.

"Hey, Logan, how's it going?" Zack asked, walking up to him.

"It's okay."

"You looking at commercial real estate? I thought you were the new gym teacher."

"I am, but it's a term position and I'm hoping to open up a gym by the time the maternity leave teacher is back. I thought this space might work."

Zack nodded. "Does it?"

"Yeah, with renovations." Logan looked back toward the building. It would be fine, but he couldn't shake the feeling that something about it didn't feel right. It was a good space, but it wasn't *his* space.

"I wish I could offer you the extra space in my shop, but somehow I don't think that'll work for you."

Logan shook his head. The area was okay, but too small

for a gym, nor would it be an appropriate place for one. The thought of people lifting weights while others shopped for a craft supplies made him chuckle.

"Can you imagine my clients working out in your store?"

"Definitely not." Zack joined him in the laugh. "Although I would love to find a way to use that section of my store. It looks so empty and wasted. I'm sure you'll find a good place for your gym. This building is great. Conveniently located in the middle of town too."

"I was hoping for somewhere with a little more parking, but this might work."

"Real estate doesn't move quickly in this town. People tend to settle in for the long haul."

"Nothing wrong with that." He'd give anything to have a place to call home, somewhere to settle and be a part of the community was what he'd always dreamed about.

"I'll let you know if I hear of any properties coming up, and if you think of anything I could add to my store to fill that space, give me a holler," Zack said, looking at his watch. "You want to grab a bite? I have Cheryl watching the store for an hour."

"Actually, I was on my way to lunch with a friend. Want to join us?" Logan walked to his car and unlocked the doors.

"Sure." Zack pulled open the passenger side door while Logan climbed in and reached to move Tessa's things from the passenger seat.

"I'll get this stuff out of the way."

Logan tossed her sweater to the backseat and was carefully moving her sketchbook when a thought occurred to him—what if Tessa used the extra space in Zack's store? She could give art classes and then the students could buy supplies from Zack. And Logan would win too because Tessa would be in town and he'd still get to date her.

He held the book on his lap while Zack climbed into the

car and shut the door. Tessa didn't usually show people her sketches, but she'd been showing her paintings to a ton of galleries trying to get a job. If he was trying to get her one with Zack, then it was reasonable to assume he could do the same, right? How else could she—or him on her behalf—get an art job without showing some kind of portfolio of work?

They couldn't.

Not to mention, her sketches were beautiful and surely he wouldn't be the only one who thought so.

"Have you ever thought about having artists do classes in your store?" Logan asked.

"No, but it's something I would definitely consider. Why? Are you offering?"

"Not for myself, but for the friend I'm meeting for lunch. She's an artist and she's pretty personable." *When she's not fighting with me.* "I bet she'd be great. Take a look at this."

Logan flipped to the sketch of the moonlight lake. Seeing it in the daylight, it was even better than he remembered. "Pretty great, right? And how about this one?" He flipped to the one of him on the paddleboard, then the view from the lookout. Each one showed a slightly different nuance but was equally as awesome.

"These are fantastic. I would definitely hire this girl to do some classes for me, at least on a trial basis. You know, see if the community is interested. I could even frame some of these and display them in the store for sale. I bet people around here would buy them. Well, maybe not that one of you, but the landscapes for sure. I can definitely see the tourists buying them. They love this kind of thing."

"That's great."

Logan drove the short distance to the diner while Zack flipped through a few more pages, thankfully missing the one of Logan naked at lookout point. No one else ever needed to see that one. His body was for Tessa's eyes only. When he pulled into the parking lot of Randy's Diner, Tessa was waiting outside the front door, sitting on the steps, looking at her phone.

"There she is. I can't wait to tell her." Logan stepped out of the car as Tessa walked up. His excitement about her new job prospect fizzled at the expression on her face.

She rounded the front of the car to the passenger side door where Zack stood, sketchbook in hand. She ripped it from his grip and clutched it to her chest. "What are you doing with that?"

"That's yours?" Zack asked. "Tessa's the artist you're talking about? No way."

"What's Zack talking about? Why does he have my book?" she asked, squaring off with Logan. "What did you do?"

Logan took a step forward, reaching for her. "I have great news." Even as his said it, he began to doubt the greatness. "Zack mentioned needing something to do with the empty space in the store and so I thought of you and suggested you give some art classes."

"You didn't," she said, her jaw clenched so tight he barely heard her say the words.

"I know you don't like to show your work to a lot of people, but this is a job opportunity so I figured you'd be okay with it. You show all the galleries in the city your other work."

Why was she so upset? It was a job, featuring her artistic abilities, and it was in town where everyone already knew her, loved her, and supported her. This was a winning situation for everyone involved.

"I had no idea you were such a great artist," Zack said. "I'd be happy to frame a few of those for you and display them in my shop."

It was as if Tessa hadn't even heard Zack speak. Her eyes were locked on Logan's. "I can't believe you showed him, of all people, my private work. How could you do that to me? How could you go behind my back like this and stick your nose in my work where it doesn't belong? I thought I could trust you."

"I didn't go behind your back. I had a conversation with someone I thought you might be able to work with. I don't understand what the big deal is."

She laughed, but it didn't sound joyful. It sounded bordering on psychotic. "You showed my work and made a business deal with my ex-boyfriend, without my consent or even the desire for such a deal mentioned in passing, and you don't see why that's a big deal. Is that what you're telling me?"

Oh no.

"Zack is your ex? I didn't…"

"Of course you didn't because you didn't bother to ask me first before you started meddling." She turned on Zack. "And you. You thought you'd play dumb with the new guy and pretend you didn't know me? What's your angle, huh? How are you planning on screwing me over this time? Are you going to say you love my work, then display it so you can show the rest of the town how terrible it is?"

"Tessa, I honestly like your work." Zack sounded genuine. "I wouldn't do that."

"Yeah right. Like you honestly wouldn't sleep around behind my back and then laugh about it with the whole town until I found out?"

"I'm sorry about that. I wish I could make it up to you, take it back."

"You're that ex?" Logan asked, realization hitting him like a sledgehammer to the chest. Now her reaction made sense. This was the guy who'd screwed her over. No wonder she didn't want to work with him. Thinking about what Zack did to her in the past made Logan's skin crawl. "Tessa, I didn't know. It's not like we exchanged personal histories."

"No. Instead you showed my private work, that I trusted you with, to basically a total stranger. You want to trap me here like everyone else does."

Logan shook his head. "It's not like that. It came up in conversation and I went with the idea. It wasn't like I planned it or anything."

Tessa's finger shook as she pointed at him, her voice rising. "It wasn't like you thought about how I'd feel about this either, did you? You had no right to do this and instead of admitting it, you're defending yourself."

"Tessa, go easy on the poor guy. He didn't know our history and I didn't know who the artist was. I swear." Zack moved toward he as if to comfort her. She backed away like a gazelle cornered by a lion. "I guess I should have recognized his name now that I think about it. Your family did a good job picking out a guy this time. His heart is definitely in the right place."

She held up her hands. "Wait a second. What did you say?"

"He's a good guy."

"Not that part." She rubbed her forehead as if she was getting a migraine. "The part about my family picking a good one."

Zack shrugged. "Well, I know I just met the guy, but he already seems a lot better for you than I ever was."

Logan put his arm around Tessa in an attempt to quell her trembling. "You're shaking."

"He knew too," she whispered. "Who else knew about Logan?"

"What?" Zack asked.

"Who else knew about Logan and me being fixed up this week during the camping trip?" she asked louder.

"I don't know. I heard it mentioned a few times, but it wasn't like the talk of the town or anything."

"I don't believe this," she said.

"I thought we'd worked through this already. You're acting like this is news, but we knew about the matchmaking plan yesterday."

"Yes *we* knew yesterday, but *the whole town* knew before that. That's what I'm talking about, Logan. That's why I need out of this place. I can't trust anyone here."

"Tessa, calm down. Let's go have some lunch and we'll figure this out." Logan tried to steer her toward the door of the diner.

"No. I'm not going anywhere with you. You don't think this is a big deal because you like that they stuck their noses in our business. You did it too, going behind my back with Zack about the art classes. You're a meddler like the rest of my family, like the rest of this town! No wonder they love you so much already. You fit in perfectly."

"Tessa, that's not fair—"

"The unfair thing is that I'm the only one who ever sees there's a problem with how this town works. I thought you were different, Logan, but you're the same as the rest of them. I'm done with everything related to Cutter's Creek, and now that includes you."

She slipped out of his arms and disappeared into her rental car while he stood there stunned and unmoving. Her words sank in like bricks. As she peeled out of the parking lot, she didn't even give him one last glance. He'd lost her, like everyone else in his life.

They'd known each other a total of six days, but it felt as if he'd been waiting for her his whole life. Now that she was gone, something inside him was missing, but he didn't go after her. He couldn't.

She'd judged him based on the actions of others and accused him of purposefully betraying and hurting her, something he'd never willingly do. If she could be so wrong about him, maybe he'd been wrong about falling for her.

Chapter Eighteen

Tessa took a slurp from her bottle of water, draining it, then tossed it to the floor of the passenger side. It didn't make a sound as it landed on the pile of crumpled, used tissues. She'd grabbed a fresh box from the cabin when she'd hastily packed her things, and now the box was empty.

So was her chest.

Once upon a time ago, she'd had a heart in that spot, but it had been replaced with a void so big she could park her rental car in it. Her family had done nothing but hurt her with this trip, tricking her into falling for Logan so she'd inevitably move home. Worse still, Logan was like the rest of them, meddling with her life so he could benefit from it. Well, it was her turn to start benefitting from her life.

Driving across the George Washington Bridge, the traffic was bumper to bumper, surrounding her on all sides. On the route back, the roads had been relatively empty except near the cities. She had to admit, she preferred the wide-open roads to the congested ones. The busier they got, the more nervous she became. By the time she hit the bridge to cross into Manhattan, her nerves were on edge and her hands were sore from gripping the steering wheel.

She was awestruck by the immensity of the city. Somehow, it seemed even bigger than the first time she'd seen it. The buildings loomed above her, making her feel small and insignificant in their vast shadows. As she pulled into the rental car place, fatigue over the marathon drive and exhaustion from crying finally took its toll. Her legs shook as she got out of the car, retrieved her belongings, and returned the keys. The night clerk barely offered her a grunted acknowledgement as she signed her name on the credit card slip.

If she'd been in Cutter's Creek, the clerk would have thanked her by name, called a friend to pick her up, and offered her a cup of coffee while she waited. Then again, if she were back home, she wouldn't need a rental. If she needed a ride and didn't have her own vehicle, someone from town would drive her wherever she needed to go. Hell, if she'd asked, someone would've driven here, picked her up to bring her camping, and returned her without so much as batting an eye at the inconvenience, because it wasn't an inconvenience — it was something you did for a neighbor.

As she walked the last few blocks to her apartment building, lugging her bags with her, the heat of late summer smothered her, draining the last of her energy. The stench of decomposing garbage washed over her in waves as she passed by the piles of black bags on the curb waiting for collection. Had it always smelled this bad in the city or was it a particularly stinky night? Regardless, the smell was overwhelming and by the time she made it into her apartment, she needed a shower. Creeping to the bathroom as quietly as she could so not to wake her three roommates, she rinsed off, put on her coziest pajamas she had, and climbed into bed.

More than anything she wanted to fall asleep after the excruciatingly long day, but sleep eluded her. Instead, her mind replayed every moment of her trip home—almost running into Logan on the way to the campground, spending time with her family, the hike, the times she'd spent in Logan's arms. By the time she'd gotten to the events of that day, her breath hitched in her chest as her body shook with tears.

Everything was a mess.

After her fight with Logan and Zack, she'd gone back to the camp and packed her things and left without even saying goodbye to her family. They'd called a couple of hours later to check on her and she'd assured them she was okay. She was anything but okay.

She'd never been less okay in her life.

Logan rolled over and stretched. He couldn't remember ever having such miserable sleep. The night had been spent tossing one direction then flipping over to the other. Every time he faced toward Tessa's empty bed, the pit in his stomach grew.

He'd taken his time getting back to the cabin after his fight with her. For a while, he'd stood around outside of Randy's Diner not knowing what the hell had happened. Finally, he'd gotten back in his car and headed for the campground, deciding that no matter where he stood with Tessa they needed to talk it out. She had to know he hadn't meant to overstep any bounds and if he had by talking to Zack, then he was sorry.

By the time he'd gotten back, she was gone, along with all of her things.

Her empty bed mocked him, reminding him of how badly he'd screwed up. Instead of going after her to fix things right away, he'd been stupid and had let her get away. Hoping she'd answer her phone any of the times he'd called had been an exercise in futility. He'd left voicemails knowing she was unlikely to listen to them. He'd texted her too. At least those he was sure she would see, whether or not she'd actually read any of them.

He dragged himself from the cocoon of his sheets and into a hot shower. Water couldn't wash away the ache settled deep into his bones like a chill on a frigid night. He hadn't even known her at this time the week before, but now he couldn't imagine this time next week without her in his life. His life had suddenly become some kind of torturous purgatory between having Tessa and losing Tessa and he had no idea where he'd eventually land.

Once out of the shower, he carelessly shoved his belongings into his bag. Little things didn't matter anymore, not when the big things in his world continued to fall apart. First he closed the doors to his dream gym, then he'd gained and lost Tessa in less than a week, and now he was stuck in a town with a bunch of people who would probably hate him for making her leave again.

He tossed his bag into his car and went into the main cabin to say goodbye. Wanting to slink away with his tail between his legs was one thing, but he wouldn't be rude enough to do it.

"You look like hell," Travis said as Logan walked into the living room.

"Thanks, man. I can always count on you to tell me the truth." Logan attempted to joke, but he lacked the needed enthusiasm or sarcasm. "I'm heading out. Are Martha and Joe around? I wanted to say thank you for having me here this week, even if it didn't end up as planned."

"They're out on the lake. I'll make sure to tell them," Sally said from her spot on the couch beside Travis. "I'm sorry things didn't work out with Tessa. We thought you two would hit it off."

"We did." Logan flopped down into a chair. "We got along great. I think that's part of the problem."

"That doesn't make any sense," Mary said, as she walked out of the kitchen with two cups of coffee in her hands. "Drink this. You need it."

He accepted the proffered coffee with gratitude.

"How can people get along too well? Either you want to bang each other or you don't. There isn't such a thing as wanting to bang too much." Travis stuffed a chunk of bagel into his mouth.

"Banging? That's so classy," Sally said, rolling her eyes.

"Hey, you're the one who married him," Mary said, laughing.

"What was I thinking?"

Logan sipped his coffee. "Tessa hated that you guys set us up and that we were a good match. She's tired of everyone trying to influence her decisions or making them for her."

"So it's our fault she left yesterday? I feel terrible." Mary twisted her hands in her lap.

"No, that honor lays solely with me," Logan said, looking down at his half empty mug.

"What did you do?" Sally asked.

"I thought I was being helpful but apparently I got her a job with her ex-boyfriend."

"Oh. Dude. That's…bad," Travis said.

"Yeah. Lesson learned."

"You've got a plan to get her back, right?" Mary asked.

He shook his head. "I wish."

"You better make it something amazing," Sally added.

"Thanks for the added pressure." Logan stood. "If you hear from her, tell her…"

"That you miss her?"

"That you're sorry?"

"That you want to bang her again?"

Logan sighed. "Tell her to answer my calls so I can say all that stuff to her myself."

L ogan filled a grocery basket with essentials—chips, dip, beer, a vegetable tray, steak, and potatoes in an attempt to have a proper meal. He hadn't really eaten much since Tessa left and regardless of his lack of appetite, he had to get back on track before starting his new job.

Every day, multiple times a day, he'd called Tessa. And every day, multiple times a day, she'd ignored him. Knowing he screwed things up with her was one thing, but not being given the opportunity to make things right was intolerable. Even if she never forgave him, he still wanted to say the words he'd been repeating in his head but refused to say to her voicemail—I love you.

He'd been surprised when the pit in his stomach wouldn't subside. Slowly the discomfort migrated through his body until it rooted in his chest and blossomed into all out heartache. The constricting pain, similar to being in a vice grip, hadn't dissipated yet. Even when he slept, he had dreams of being squeezed in the tight coils of a boa constrictor or sandwiched between two tectonic plates.

He added a bottle of ibuprofen to this basket, the kind that had the PM behind the name because it included a mild sedative. Hopefully it would let him relax enough to knock him out for a night of good sleep before he started work in a few days.

"Mrs. Matherson, how are you today?" he asked, purposefully using her name. It was a technique he used at school too. He always tried to use people's names to commit them to memory faster and so the person felt a connection with him.

"I'm okay, Logan. How are you settling in?" she asked, taking each item out of his basket and scanning it.

As they came down the short conveyor belt, he bagged them. "Mostly settled in now. Starting at the school on Monday."

"Have you had any luck with Tessa yet?"

He knew it would annoy Tessa to know he was talking about her personal life, but he needed to talk to someone and his options were limited. "No. I keep calling and texting, but she's ignoring me."

"Have you tried sending flowers? Her favorites are irises. It was her grandmother's name. Maybe you should try sending her some of those?"

"Thanks for the suggestion. Maybe I will."

Would it help win her back to send her a bouquet of flowers? How would he explain knowing which ones were her favorites? Surely the thrill of receiving them would be short-lived once she realized he'd learned that tidbit of information about her from someone in town. As much as he wanted whatever edge the insider tip would bring him, he wasn't willing to risk inadvertently crossing that line again between her private life and the rest of the town. Any gesture he made would have to come from his doing only.

Chapter Nineteen

It had been twenty-four hours since Tessa's last big snot-filled cry. She took it as a personal accomplishment and a sign she was finally getting over everything that had happened with Logan. Sure, it had taken a week, but progress was progress. Maybe today she'd be able to get on with her life and with her plans.

All week she'd been trying to convince herself she did, in fact, have plans, despite what reality felt like. She had hundreds, maybe even thousands of galleries to query, and she'd only contacted a fraction of those so far. Now was the perfect time to get back on track.

After a quick shower, she dressed and even put on a coat of mascara. If she looked ready to take on the world, maybe she'd start to actually feel that way too. Maybe she'd apply the same principal of thought to her portfolio. If she wanted a fresh start with the galleries, maybe she should give her portfolio a fresh makeover. Pulling the large black case out from behind her closet door, she flipped it open and examined the first piece—a watercolor of the Empire State Building.

Simple, elegant, and lit by the rays of the sun reflecting off the metal façade so it practically glowed. It was beautiful, but it was also somewhat ordinary and not that different than what she'd seen someone selling on the corner of Fifth Avenue and Forty-second Street for fifteen dollars.

Huh.

Maybe that wasn't the best one to start her portfolio with after all. Not horrendous, but certainly nothing special either. It lacked that certain indescribable quality that turned a painting into a masterpiece. Pulling it from her portfolio case, she set it aside on the floor, out of the way so she could focus on the others.

The next painting also seemed to lack something that set it apart. She felt the same about the next three. No wonder galleries wouldn't give her a job—her cityscape paintings were boring.

After flipping through the whole portfolio, she was left with only four paintings that she thought had merit. All of them happened to focus on people—playing in the park, walking a bunch of dogs, eating a hotdog, and cuddling on a park bench while children played on the swings. These ones had heart and substance. They told a story. As good as she thought these paintings were, they weren't enough. Four pieces did not make for a sufficient portfolio to show prospective galleries.

Her sketchbook still sat on top of the dresser where she'd left it when she'd gotten back from camping. She hadn't looked in it since, not wanting to be reminded of her time with Logan. Now it beckoned to her, begging her to reach for it. All week Logan had told her how much he loved her drawings, but he wasn't an artist so what did he know?

One of the last pages she'd used had been the moonlit night they'd sat on the dock and talked. She'd been so comfortable with him that night. Everything had felt so right between them, so easy, as if each of them made up a half of a whole when they were together.

That night she'd learned about his gym. He'd taken a risk opening it and then had to shut it down because the city was too hard, too challenging, and he'd struggled as long as he could. But instead of completely giving up, he'd made a new plan, switched gears and thought of something different he could do to make his dream a reality.

Logan was a survivor. He persevered where others would've given up. He'd tried to help her figure out how she could too. Instead of listening, she'd brushed him off. What if he was right? What if what she needed was a new twist on her art career?

Comparing the moonlit night sketch to her Empire State Building painting, the two pieces were about as different as they could possibly be. One was warm, comforting, and so full of emotional depth that it practically oozed with the sounds of nighttime creatures and water lapping at the shore. The other was cold, hard-edged, flat, and silent.

She'd been so in love with the idea of being in the city that she hadn't realized how little love there was in her cityscapes. She'd thought she'd captured the essence of the city in each painting, but all she'd done was draw a picture of a building. Her pictures from home were all heart and storytelling. Each one gave her a tiny peek into life in Cutter's Creek—a life that was full of warmth, love, hospitality, and community.

Damn it. She'd been so stupid.

Without thinking too deeply about how much she might make a fool of herself, she called her top gallery and asked for another meeting. He'd asked to see other work and now she could offer that to him. With her appointment scheduled, she carefully selected the best drawings from her week back home and added them to her portfolio.

A spike of excitement shot through her. This time she

wouldn't fail.

Logan stood on the side of the gym clapping and cheering the fifth graders on as they tried to dribble basketballs up and down the court before taking shots at the net. Most balls rolled away or were kicked by clumsy feet. Almost none made it into the basket, but he didn't care. They were learning the sport, having fun, and getting some much needed exercise in their otherwise stationary school day.

It had been two weeks and he'd settled in nicely to the new school. Sure, it wasn't as good as having hours he created, but it wasn't terrible either. School ended at three and then he was free to do what he wanted for the rest of the day. Of course, most days that had consisted of a workout then lazing around his small apartment trying to figure out how to get Tessa back. So far, his plans totaled zero.

The buzzer rang signaling the change in classes. This batch of kids would leave and he'd get a new one. Every thirty-five minutes the same thing happened.

"Okay everyone," he called, clapping his hands to get their attention. "Toss the balls back into the bins and line up by the door."

The children did as they were told while he stood in front of the doors where they'd file out and the next class would file in. "What do you have next, Michelle?" he asked one of the girls near the front of the line.

"Ugh. Art. I hate art."

"Really? I thought that was usually one of the favorite subjects at school."

"Maybe if you're good at art, but if you suck, like I do, then the class is the worst."

"I'm positive you don't suck at art, Michelle. What are you

guys doing in class right now?" he asked, while also waving at the last few kids to hurry up. They had to go as a group to their next room. He couldn't let them leave until he had each one accounted for.

"We're drawing birds," Tom said. "Really stupid birds."

"Yeah, they wouldn't let us draw anything else. Just birds," Robby added.

"Try your best. It's the heart you put into your drawing that makes it special, not the perfect technique." With the last two kids now in line, he opened the door and shooed them down the hall to their next class. "See you next week."

As he reset his gym for the next group, he thought about the kid's bird art. They had to be better artists than he was. He could barely draw a stick bird. There'd been a couple of birds in Tessa's book. They'd been great, of course. That girl could draw anything and make it incredible.

An idea hit him like a basketball to the forehead. Maybe he should take the advice he'd given the kids and put his heart into a few drawings of his own. He'd managed to lose Tessa by showing off her private sketchbook to Zack, so maybe he could win her back by showing her one of his.

The rest of the day went by in a blur of children coming and going from his gym. He was with it enough to instruct them and make sure none of them hurt themselves, but while he stood clapping and cheering, his mind was formulating a plan. By the time the last bell rang for the day, he had a list of supplies he needed and immediately went to Zack's hobby shop.

He searched the aisles, finding each of the items he needed and was headed to the checkout when Zack wandered up.

"That a gift for Tessa? Hoping to win her back with art supplies?" Zack asked.

Logan wanted to share his plan and get Zack's opinion, but if there was one thing he knew drove Tessa crazy, it was the town people finding out about her life before she did. He wouldn't make the same mistake.

"No. These are for me actually. I thought I might do some drawing this weekend."

Not a lie, but not the whole truth either.

"I thought you weren't an artist."

"I'm not, but I'm trying to be." He paid for his supplies and said a quick goodbye, making plans for the following week to meet up to watch one of the games on the big screen at the bar since he still hadn't made it there yet.

Back at his apartment, he set up all his necessary supplies, grabbed a drink and a sandwich, and got started. He'd work all weekend if he had to.

Tessa wouldn't return his calls and he had no idea if she'd read his texts. Surely she would open a couriered package. When she did, she'd open the cover, not only to his sketchbook for her, but to his heart, his life—everything he wanted to share with her. Hopefully it would be enough to start a conversation with her. After that, he'd do anything to earn a future with her, even if it meant giving up everything he was building in Cutter's Creek. He loved it here, but it wasn't the same without her and with total clarity he knew he'd do anything if it meant getting her back.

He'd even move to the city because with her there he'd always feel like he was home.

Tessa tried not to fiddle in her seat while Darren Pembroke of Pembroke Gallery looked over her new and improved portfolio. It had taken a week to get another appointment with him. This was it, her last chance. If she couldn't do it with two meetings, she'd never get a third.

"These are great. I'm impressed with your skill and

technique." Darren looked up from the portfolio case. "I do have one concern."

"What is it?" she asked, sitting on the edge of her seat.

"I don't understand why you didn't show me these drawings before. They're far superior to the work you showed me last time. Why didn't I get to see these at our last meeting?"

What could she say? She hadn't shown him because she thought they were crap and because she was trying to dump her old small town life for a new big city one. She couldn't tell him the real reason she'd kept them from him. What if it made him distrust her judgment on what constituted good work over bad? "I was recently back home in Cutter's Creek and that's where I did most of those. They simply didn't exist at the time of our first meeting."

That sounded good.

"All of these were done recently? How long did each one take?"

What was the right answer he'd be looking for? She had no idea so went with the truth. "Some were as little as thirty minutes. Those ones usually have less detail. The others took closer to an hour."

"That's truly astonishing. With that kind of output, you could fill a gallery space within weeks." His eyes seemed to sparkle with a hint of excitement.

"I suppose I could. A gallery this size I could probably fill in about three weeks, if I was asked to." Her hint wasn't exactly subtle.

"I think we could do that. I have an opening in a month. I think we could definitely get these framed in that amount of time if you can produce the work."

"I can get started today. I'll grab a map and hit the city, sketching as I go."

"Oh no. I think there's been a miscommunication." Darren shook his head and sat back, folding his arms across his chest. "I don't want to see anymore cityscapes."

"Oh... Okay. What would you like to see?"

"I want more like these—landscapes, small town life, nature. All of it is great. I don't want any tall buildings, concrete sidewalks, or yellow taxicabs. Can you do that?"

Could she? The more she looked at her sketches from home, the more she liked them. They gave her a sense of peace and tranquility, and made her feel like she was surrounded by the warmth of invisible arms hugging her. Could she capture the spirit of home while still living in the city? Would her memories be enough or would she have to visit home more often as a business trip for inspiration?

"I've got another meeting in five minutes. Why don't you take some time to think about my offer, the timing and the kind of work I'm looking for and get back to me?" He stood from the table and offered his hand.

She stood and shook it then quickly gathered her things. "Great. Thank you so much for the offer. I'll be in touch soon."

Tessa walked out with her head in a fog. She'd had no idea her landscapes would be so well received, and by her top gallery no less. This was the opportunity she'd been waiting for, if she could make it work. She'd wanted to escape life in Cutter's Creek, but it seemed that wasn't meant to be. It was her home, her inspiration, but surely it didn't mean she had to live there to draw it. She could finally have everything she'd wanted—live in the city and be a successful artist.

She grabbed a coffee and found a table on the outside patio to sit and revel in her gallery offer. Finding a clean sheet of paper and a charcoal pencil, she closed her eyes and put herself back on lookout point. It didn't matter if she was sitting in Manhattan. The views of the Appalachian Mountains were forever burned in her brain in rich detail. She'd been immersed in that setting since birth. She thought about the wind on her face, warm and comforting like Logan's touch.

No. She didn't want to include him in her thoughts.

Colors. The colors of the mountain range changed throughout the day. During the bright sunlight-filled morning there were hues of greens and brown, like when Logan and her hiked to the lookout. Other times there were purples and dark blues, like when they watched the sunset over the treetops and the shadows lengthened from twilight to darkness. What did the trees in Cutter's Creek look like in today's dying light?

Her heart suddenly ached at the thought of her hometown.

Opening her eyes to release the memories, she put her pencil to the page and drew, trying to block out everything else around her and focus only on the landscape she wanted to create. More slowly than usual, the picture took shape. It was a little rough around the edges, but it was there. With more practice, she could totally draw scenes from back home while still here.

She sipped her coffee hoping the feeling of triumph and satisfaction at having completed her first landscape while in the city would hit her soon.

Traffic whooshed by mere feet from her chair since she was basically sitting at a table on the sidewalk. But that was part of the charm, right? Everyone else didn't seem to mind the vehicle exhaust that went along with an afternoon coffee break, nor did they mind the heat radiating off the pavement, or the constant white noise of traffic and conversations. If she listened really hard, she could hear a bird chirping in the distance.

A passerby bumped her table and her coffee sloshed out of her cup and onto the corner of her newest sketch. *Well, that one was only for practice anyway*, she thought, carefully dabbing up the liquid. A brown stain remained. This was totally what she wanted—bustling city life where no one paid attention to her. Her heart sank.

If she had everything she wanted, why did she still feel like a part of her was missing? If being in the city was this amazing experience, why did she miss the quiet tree-lined streets of Cutter's Creek when she'd tried so hard to get out of that town? Why wasn't she happy?

Chapter Twenty

A package leaned against the door to Tessa's apartment. Ignoring it for a minute, she let herself in and went straight to her room, dumping her portfolio onto the bed. She'd dragged that thing around all day while looking for different, inspirational sketching areas to work, but had finally conceded defeat and came back to the apartment.

Retrieving the package, she checked the name to see what bed to put it on this time. Her roommates loved to shop online. There were constantly packages waiting at their door. Either they somehow had endless amounts of disposable income, or they had enormous credit card bills.

To: Ms. Tessa Cutter.

Huh. She hadn't ordered anything.

From: Cutter's Creek.

The return address wasn't a house or business. It was simply the address of the post office. *Weird.*

Placing it gently on her bed, she paced around her tiny room, eyeing it as if it might detonate. What if it was from him? But if it was, why wouldn't it have his address on it? Was this another trick? What if it wasn't a trick but a gift? A "we miss you but we're happy you're following your dream" gift from the town? It was the kind of thing they'd do.

Perching on the edge of the mattress, she ripped the paper to find a decorative box. It was beautiful with a cream colored background covered in purple irises. Without hesitating, she lifted the lid, suddenly eager to see what was inside.

Her breath caught in her throat as she pulled out a light blue book, *Our Story* written across the cover. Leaning back against her wall, she set the book in her lap and flipped it open.

The first page made her giggle instantly. Two terribly drawn cars were on the side of a winding road. They looked like they'd been drawn by school children, yet somehow she knew they hadn't been. It was as if she could feel Logan's presence on the page, specifically crafting each tiny detail, like the way she'd worn her hair that day and the color of the mystery fluid leaking from her car.

She bit her lip to stem off the tears threatening to fall and flipped the page. This one depicted a girl with her naked back visible; a curvy W attached to two stick legs highlighted the girl's ass. There were bubbles in her hair, and a spider on her back. She laughed and shivered at the same time, reliving the memory. The stick man in the picture had one hand on her butt while the other slapped at the spider. An additional line clearly illustrated his enthusiasm at the predicament he'd found himself in.

Logan hadn't done himself justice. His real stick was definitely bigger. Girthier.

"I can't believe he did this for me," she said to herself. While his artistic talent might only be at a third-grade level, his effort and dedication to the project were clearly over the top. The project must've taken him hours to complete. Each page was a like a new gift intended only for her with moments they shared together. By the middle of the book, tears flowed freely down her cheeks and she stopped bothering to wipe them away.

He was an amazing man. And she'd left him. She'd thrown away the best thing in her life because he'd tried to do something nice for her and she'd overreacted. Yet, he'd still gone to the trouble of making her this incredible gift. She didn't deserve him, but damn it, she loved him.

Everything about him was more than she'd ever hoped to find in a man. He was attractive, kind, and funny. He could make her more annoyed and angry than anyone else, but he also made her happier and more at peace than she ever remembered being before.

He'd been patient, and persistent. She loved him. Every single thing about him. And she'd screwed it up. Was it too late to get him back?

Tessa flipped to the last page of the book and gasped as fresh tears blurred her vision so badly she had to take a moment to wipe them away. There they were, embracing, in what had to be a stick version of Central Park with a message in his handwriting scrawled across the grass— *You followed your dreams and stole my heart along the way. I was wrong. I don't need the small town life. I only need the small town girl in my life.*

He'd put himself and his heart out there for her to see with this book. He'd offered to give up everything he was building in her hometown. But she couldn't let him do that, not after everything he'd already done for her. She needed to go back to be with him. No, she *wanted* to go back. The difference between obligation and desire suddenly made her future crystal clear.

Now she needed a plan to make her future a reality.

"Pembroke Gallery," the voice on the other end of the line said in a cheery tone. Tessa hoped the first stage of her plan would be accepted. If it wasn't, then she'd have to go to plan B, except that she didn't have one.

"Can I speak with Mr. Pembroke, please? It's Tessa Cutter."

"One moment."

She twirled a strand of her hair as she waited. If he said no, what would she do? Give up her dream if it meant getting Logan back? Yes. She was prepared to do that. But damn, she didn't want it to come to that.

"Miss. Cutter. Have you made your decision? I hope you've decided to work with us. I already have customers in mind for some of your pieces."

He did? Fantastic!

"I have." She took a deep breath to calm her racing heart. "I'd love to work with your gallery."

"Excellent news. I'll get you on the schedule for that opening we discussed at our meeting. I assume with the speed you mentioned you'll have enough pieces done by then?"

"Well, I hope with the right inspiration, I will."

"Great!"

"But that's something else I wanted to speak with you about. I'd like to work where my inspiration is, which would mean leaving New York. It would also mean that I wouldn't be available all the time to meet with customers. Or you. But," she added quickly before he thought she was brushing him off entirely. "I'd be happy to come back for gallery nights."

"Every couple of months we host a night where customers are able to chat with the artists. I would also need you to be present at those. No exceptions."

She smiled and fist-pumped the air, thankful that this was a phone conversation and not in person so he couldn't see her. "I can do that."

"Have twenty-five pieces to me in three weeks so I can have them framed."

She took down the details of how and where to ship her pieces to the gallery, as well as the date and time of her gallery opening and her first Meet the Artists night. By the time she got off the phone call, her brain was swimming in the "I can't believe this is actually happening" pond, which was vastly different than the last pond she went swimming in. With Logan. Naked.

Logan…

Time to start stage two of her plan for getting him back. First things first, she had to swallow her pride and make a call to the one person who could help her orchestrate everything. She dialed and tapped her fingers on her knee while waiting for the voice she'd been missing more than she wanted to admit. The moment she heard the familiar "hello" a wave of relief and comfort washed over her, erasing the mistakes she'd made lately.

"Mom, I'm moving home and I need your help."

Logan checked his cell phone again for the hundredth time. Tessa still hadn't called or texted. Nothing since the day she'd left him standing in the parking lot of Randy's Diner. The day his fresh start had turned sour. The woman he loved was gone. If only he could get her to listen to him long enough to tell her how he felt.

The tracking on his package said it had been delivered a week and a half ago, so she must've opened it and looked inside by now, so why hadn't she reached out to him? Forgiven him? Or hell, talked to him long enough to tell him to take a leap off a bridge.

He couldn't take the silent treatment anymore. It was

slowly killing him. Every day felt like torture. If he wasn't a teacher, with kids depending on him to be there each day, he'd have already driven back to New York to find her. But he couldn't run off like that. He had responsibilities to the kids here, and he wasn't about to let his personal life affect his work.

He would've gone back to New York for her. His offer on the last page of the sketchbook he'd created had been true. She had to know that, didn't she? So that only left one option—she didn't want him there.

He had no choice but to move on, as sad as his future looked right now.

The gym space he'd looked at a few weeks ago had been sold to one of the locals. Some guy who decided he needed an actual storefront for his architecture business. Apparently some of the tourists who usually came and went with the seasons had decided to stay and his home design business had suddenly grown.

The other place he hoped would come on the market had for a day, or so he was told. He'd never actually gotten to see the listing. Last week someone made the owner an offer they couldn't refuse. He assumed someone from town had decided to rent the space since the owner hadn't liked the thought of an "outsider" taking over. He'd already seen construction going on but everyone he'd asked didn't seem to know any of the details. How they knew what he'd eaten for lunch that day but didn't know what was going into that space was beyond him.

But he wasn't getting discouraged. When his teaching gig was over, if he still didn't have a space to call his own, then he was starting an outdoor gym. Sure, it wouldn't have any fancy equipment or facilities but he would still offer people a great workout. As an added benefit to not having rent, he'd be able to charge people only a small fee per class. He'd already found a nice park by the lake for a yoga class and another park in the middle of town that had a track where he could run a boot camp style class.

It wasn't what he originally envisioned, or his dream gym, but it was a start. Maybe the more people who started training with him, the more he'd be accepted in town. At some point maybe someone would even rent him a space.

Logan flopped down on the couch with a pile of mail in his hands. A vanilla colored envelope caught his eye. The writing across the front was informal and cheery, making him think of birthday parties or barbeques.

Sliding out the postcard, it took a minute to realize what he was looking at. It was an invitation all right, to a grand opening of a new business—the business with all the construction last week that no one seemed to know anything about.

Join us for the grand opening of Body & Mind Studio *for an evening guaranteed to make you hot and dirty. Casual attire recommended.*

Well, that was about the weirdest invitation he'd ever received. The party was today, in an hour. The last thing he was in the mood for was a party, but he couldn't resist the temptation of finding out what business had gotten the property he'd been eyeing. Decision made—he'd go.

Tessa bit her fingernails while she paced in front of the closed doors. A curtain had been draped across the windows and door in an effort to keep people from seeing what was going on inside before the big reveal. Of course, it also meant she couldn't see if he was out there.

He'd come, wouldn't he?

Why wouldn't he? What else was there to do in town

tonight? Nothing. She'd made sure of that.

"Stop biting your nails, Tessa-bear," her mother said, coming to her side. She'd been Tessa's right hand for the last week, coordinating and scheduling the onsite work as well as the deliveries of needed supplies and equipment.

After a long, long week of working overtime on both this project and her pieces for Pembroke, she was exhausted, nervous, and excited. Mostly, she was anxious to see Logan again. She purposefully hadn't responded to him after making her decision, but now she feared she'd broken contact with him for too long. What if he'd thought she was over him so he'd gotten over *her*? What if he hated that she went behind his back and created this place? If the tables were turned, she'd probably be pissed.

"I can't help it," she said, nibbling on another nail. "I'm so nervous."

"Don't be, sis," James said, coming to her other side. "The place turned out great. I think the town will like it."

She didn't care what the town thought. Only one opinion mattered—Logan's.

"It's time," her father said, walking to the front door. James and Travis each gripped one of the curtains, ready to pull them down on her signal.

She took a deep breath, hoped this had been the right way to show Logan how she felt, and gave the signal. All at once, the curtains fell allowing the evening sun to stream in through the windows, lighting the space behind her. Her father opened the door and Tessa walked out to the cheers of her friends and neighbors, people who had always been there to support her, even when she didn't appreciate it or deserve it. This was why people lived in small towns. She'd been too stupid to realize it earlier.

"Thank you all for coming tonight and to everyone who helped me get this place together in such a short amount of time. I couldn't have done it without you." She paused while everyone clapped.

Her eyes scanned the crowd. Near the back and off to one side Logan stood staring at her as if she were a mirage in the desert sun. Tears stung her eyes but she blinked them away. Seeing him again was so much harder than she'd expected. Fear that he'd reject her threatened to overwhelm her.

"Invite them in, dear," her mother whispered behind her. "Don't leave them standing around out there all evening."

Tessa cleared her throat and tried to remember what she wanted to say next. "I invited you here for the grand opening of a new, and hopefully successful business in town. Of course, every business needs an owner so I need to do something. Logan, would you join me up here?"

An expression of complete shock washed over his face as he slowly made his way through the crowd. When he got to where she stood, he looked as if he might hug her, but didn't. The gesture, if she'd read it right, was encouraging. Maybe he hadn't changed his mind about her yet.

"Tessa," he said, reaching out to stroke his fingers along her jaw as if he didn't believe she was there.

Tessa took his hand in hers. "I'm back."

"For good?" His voice sounded hopeful.

"I think so, depending on how this goes, of course." She motioned to the opened doors.

"What is this exactly?" he asked.

"I hate having everyone in town knowing my business, but this time I want them to hear what I have to say. No more trying to shut people out. Including you. Because... I love you, Logan." A collective gasp came from the gathered crowd and she felt her cheeks burn hot. Public displays of affection weren't her thing, but neither was this small town she'd decided to finally call home again. "I've loved you since practically the first moment I met you."

"You mean when I almost killed you by driving you off the side of a mountain?" he asked, grinning.

"Yes, since then." She nudged him in the shoulder. "And I'm sorry I ran back to New York instead of staying here and dealing with everything."

"I'm sorry I showed Zack your sketchbook. I thought I was being helpful, but you're right, I was actually trying to find a way to keep you here. I already loved you, Tessa, and I didn't want to see you leave." He kissed her and the crowd watching them melted away. The only thing she noticed was how good his lips felt pressed to hers. "I can be a trainer anywhere, and as long as I'm with you, I'll be happy no matter where we are."

"We don't have to go anywhere. This is our new business, if you want to share the space with me. It's half gym and half art studio."

"Are you serious?" He peered inside the doors, his eyes wide.

She put a key in his palm. "Your name is on the lease with mine for a year. However, if you hate this idea, I can pull a few strings with the owner and get you out of it. Or if you love it, we can put in an offer to buy."

"Being a Cutter in this town comes with a few perks, doesn't it?" he asked.

"It doesn't hurt." She shrugged. "We can work out all the details later, but first maybe we should let everyone go in and see it. They look like they're getting restless."

"Good idea." He nodded. "I want to talk to you without an audience anyway."

She addressed the gathered crowd again. "Everyone, welcome to *Body & Mind Studio* where you can come to workout on your own or get personal training from the owner himself, Logan. Upstairs, you'll find my new art studio where I'll be holding classes for kids and adults throughout the month. Today, feel free to go upstairs and get a little dirty working with my supplies, or try out some exercises and get a little sweaty."

Everyone cheered and said congratulations on their way inside, until it was only Logan and Tessa left on the sidewalk.

"Don't you want to go in and see it too?" she asked.

"In a minute. I'm more concerned with what's going on out here." He cupped her jaw in his hands. "Are you actually staying?"

"I am." For the first time ever she felt confident in her decision, one she'd made by herself, without anyone else's influence.

"What happened with New York? Didn't you find a gallery to work with?" Concern furrowed his brow.

She smiled. "I did. I signed with Pembroke."

"That's great. So what are you doing here then?"

"I got your book. I love it. I decided living in the city wasn't important anymore. I'd rather be here with you. I'm hoping your message still applies to being here instead of in New York. Still need the small town girl even if she's in the small town?"

"I can adjust." He pulled her close. "Are you really okay moving back? I was serious when I said I'd move to the city to be with you."

"I'm sure. Coming home for the camping trip made me realize Cutter's Creek was better than I remembered and going back to the city was way worse. I thought I liked the hustle and bustle of New York, but once I was in it again, I didn't. In fact, I hated it. I finally understood what you meant about being able to take a deep breath and appreciate the open spaces."

"Well, whatever your reasons, I'm glad you're here and that you're staying." He scrunched up his forehead. "Speaking of staying, where have you been staying? You didn't get here and manage all this today, right?"

"I've been here a week or so," she said.

"And the town kept your secret the whole time?" he asked.

She nodded. "Apparently they *do* know how to do that."

He laughed. "Did you get an apartment or move back in with your parents?"

"I've been staying in my old room."

"How's that going?"

"I need to find an apartment, like yesterday."

"Move in with me." It wasn't a question so much as a request.

"Really? Doesn't it feel a little too soon in our relationship to be living together already?" she asked, wanting to say yes, but not wanting to rush into anything either.

He laughed. "Well, if we can be business partners, I'm pretty sure we can cohabitate."

The enormity of what she'd signed on for this past week suddenly hit her, but instead of feeling trapped, she was filled with calm anticipation of what would come next.

"I love you, Logan, and I'd love to move in with you, but first let's go see if you like your new gym. It could be a deal breaker if you hate it."

He took her hand and together they walked into their new business. Halfway through the room, he stopped and touched a piece of exercise equipment. "It's everything I hoped for. Better. How did you know what I wanted?"

"That night out on the dock you told me all about your plans for the gym and you seemed to love the drawing I did, so I based the real thing off that and hoped for the best."

"This place is perfect. You're perfect. But how did you ever get the money to do all of this?"

She shrugged and smirked. "Mr. Leeson from the bank never gave me a graduation gift so he decided to cut me some slack on a loan. The payments are very reasonable…for the next fifty years, or so."

He swept her into his arms and kissed her like they weren't standing in a room full of her family, friends, and neighbors.

In that moment, everything was right in her world. She finally had her art career started, her family was finally content with her life choice, and she'd fallen madly in love with a man who loved her just as much.

She'd finally found her happiness—right in Cutter's Creek.

Acknowledgments

Thank you to my agent Jill Marsal and my editor at Entangled Alethea Spiridon Hopson. Your continued belief in my stories keeps me doing what I love! I couldn't ask to work with a better team of people. You're both awesome!

Thank you to my husband Mike. Without you, I wouldn't be the person I am today. Your support and encouragement keeps me going even when things get tough. And your continued enthusiasm for crock-pot meals is deeply appreciated, especially when I'm on deadline. XOXO

About the Author

Heather Thurmeier is a lover of strawberry margaritas, a hater of spiders, and a reality TV junkie. Born and raised in the Canadian prairies, she now lives in New York with her husband and kids where she's become some kind of odd Canuck-Yankee hybrid. When she's not busy taking care of the kids and pets, Heather's writing her next romance, which will probably be filled with sassy heroines, sexy heroes who will make your heart pound, laugh out loud moments, and always a happily ever after. She loves to hear from readers on social media and her website!

Also by Heather Thurmeier...

THE WEDDING HOAX

Wedding gown designer Daisy Willows is desperate for an influx of cash to cover her mother's homecare bills. With subscriptions to his father's wedding magazine plummeting, playboy Cole Benton needs to find a way to stimulate sales, and *fast*. But then a renowned bridal show expo owner offers to bail them out—*if* they rekindle their failed relationship and plan the fake wedding of the century. Except, with all the ring shopping and kissing upon request, they're having a hard time remembering that their big white wedding is a big white *lie*...

THE HOOKUP HOAX